MAN ON A CROSS

LOUIS PROUD

CHUCK VALENTINE

"Foxes have holes, and birds of the air have nests, but the Son of Man has nowhere to lay his head."
— MATTHEW 8:20

For the one who did the heavy lifting

First edition published by Chuck Valentine February 2022

Cover design by Mykola Shelepa

ISBN (print): 978-0-6452096-3-1

ISBN (eBook): 978-0-6452096-4-8

1

WHAT PROMPTED ME TO go to church I have no idea. Perhaps I was merely bored that day. Perhaps I was feeling lost in life. Perhaps it was brought on by a brief case of insanity. Perhaps it was all three. Or maybe, just maybe, it was divinely inspired, precisely as the Christians believed, a desperate attempt on the part of God to save my troubled soul.

In any case, to church I went on that cold Sunday morning. It was one of those new Pentecostal churches. You know the sort: smartly designed, if not a little plain. Lots of polished wood and shiny surfaces. A coffee machine in the foyer. The people all happy and brimming with energy, both young and old wearing excessive grins. Mainly families with lots of kids, but more than a few single people too. Some of them guys like myself—shy, ill at ease, socially awkward, approaching middle-age. The cynic inside me wondered: were they truly Christian or had they come to Church to meet women?

If the latter, I could not blame them; the Christian girls were stunning. Beauties with long, flowing hair, smooth skin, and sensual lips. Freshly scented creatures in floral skirts. Starry-eyed, passionate lovers of Jesus, clasping their Bibles close to their breasts. A welcome contrast to the women I'd dated following my divorce: skanks with daddy issues and troubled pasts, covered in tattoos and piercings, good for nothing more than a brief relationship focused around drinking and sex, if that.

I couldn't avoid the thought: having in my life a sweet Christian woman with a respectable name like Elizabeth or Hanna might be the very thing the doctor ordered; might be the very thing to fix me.

I watched the worshippers gather in readiness to head into the auditorium. Rather than wait with them, I held back, standing off to the side near a stack of chairs, my arms folded.

The distinctive sound of mellow Christian rock drifted through the closed doors. The band was rehearsing, warming up. I manage to catch a few snippets of lyrics from the chorus: *"You're a Good, Good Father. It's who you are...It's who you are..."*

I had specifically sought out a Pentecostal church in order to be among a hipper, younger crowd; and I'd done enough research on the Pentecostals to know that they enjoyed singing and dancing to bad rock music with corny lyrics. This I didn't particularly mind. Perhaps the bad music was preferrable to the long, droning sermons found in other churches?

Suddenly I heard a voice to my right: "And who might you be, good sir?"

I spun around, a little startled. So far—to the best of my knowledge—I'd managed to blend in. Yet it seems the Christians were already onto me. The bastards were quick to recognise a new face.

He stood there smiling, a short, fiftyish, grey-haired man, with large, wistful brown eyes. Over his button-up shirt he wore a yellow vest with the words "Door Staff" emblazoned across it. He offered me his hand and we shook. "I'm Wayne. Nice to meet you."

"I'm Chuck. Chuck Valentine."

"Well, Mr. Valentine, I'm sure you'll feel right at home here. We're always pleased to see a new face. If there's anything you need, or any way I can help, please let me know. That's what I'm here for."

He was about to walk off when suddenly he paused, handing me a card from a stack in his hand. "Oh, by the way, this is good for one free coffee." He pointed towards the coffee machine. "First time visitors get one on the house."

I thanked him, placing the card in my jacket pocket.

The doors of the auditorium were open now, and the worshippers were spilling in. I waited for the majority of seats to fill before entering myself. The back row remained all but empty. It was here that I chose to park my backside. A private spot, perfect for a Doubting Thomas like myself.

For the next twenty minutes the lights remained dimmed as the band played on stage. Apart from the singer, a bald guy with a goatee and a cross tattooed on his wrist, there were four of them in total, all male, all young, and all fashionably dressed: a lead guitarist, a bassist, a drummer, and a keyboardist. It was the drummer who stood out the most. A bearded islander in his early-twenties, dressed in a tight white t-shirt that accentuated his muscular chest, he was the kind of dude teenage girls would drop their panties for in a heartbeat.

These guys weren't naïve. They were smart and slick. With their clothing and overall appearance, they'd managed to cultivate a certain image, an image that seemed to say: *"I'm a wholesome Christian guy. I love Jesus, but don't you dare take me for a square or a pushover—I've also got a bit of an edge."*

The majority of worshippers stood, some with their hands raised in the air, swaying to the rhythm of the music. Positioned at the very front, out in the open, was a tall, spider-like man wearing thick glasses. His bald head glistened under the stage lights. Though probably in his fifties, he wore skinny jeans and a black V-neck sweater. Out of everyone present, it was he who had his arms stretched out the highest. Occasionally he'd jump like a Maasai warrior, causing the crucifix around his neck to swing wildly. What was he trying to do, I wondered? Reach heaven?

As the music began to fade out with the closing of the final song, the bald guy in the V-neck took the mic and mounted the steps to the podium, a noticeable bounce in his step. So this must be the pastor, I thought. No wonder he'd been the most visibly enthusiastic of all the worshippers—he was obliged to put on a good show of faith.

He wore a wide, goofy smile as he traversed the stage, not once averting his eyes from his congregation. The entire time he said nothing, playing the room, building tension. A few nervous peals of laughter escaped from the crowd.

Finally he stood in one spot; then he spoke: "Welcome everyone. So good to see you all. Praise Jesus!"

"Praise Jesus," repeated a couple of people in the front row.

The pastor's expression morphed from happy to pensive, and in response the room went quiet. He looked down at his feet, then raised his eyes, then spoke again. "I recently witnessed what I can only describe as a miracle... Spoke to a cousin of mine recently. Not a Christian. He's sceptical of anything religious or spiritual. Believes only in science. We don't normally talk theology. On this occasion, though, he came to me with a question about God. 'Simon,' he asked, 'I need your help with something.'"

There was a long pause as the pastor gazed out at the audience. The room was uncomfortably silent; not so much as a cough or a sniffle could he heard.

"So I said to him, 'What's your question.' He asked, 'How can you believe in a loving God when there's so much suffering in the world?' Now I should mention: my cousin's had a difficult life. His father died when he was young, and his mother never fully recovered from the loss. She had problems of her own. Drinking, drugs, depression. You name it. At the age of five, he was put into foster care. He grew up feeling unloved and abandoned, an orphan. He grew up believing that no one, not even God, had his back."

I detected a few murmurs of sympathy among the parishioners, mainly from the women.

"Now, I won't relate the entire conversation. It was very intimate. We talked about his father, the father he never really knew. But we also talked about his other father, our Heavenly Father. And for the first time in his life, my cousin—the sceptic, the doubter—truly wanted to hear the Good News."

"Praise the lord!" said one elderly lady.

"Hallelujah!" said another.

The pastor continued: "There are those among us—people much like my cousin—who struggle to accept God into their heart. They push him away because they fail to see that we're not truly alone in this life; that God, our heavenly father, loves us as his children. So today, I'd like us to spend a moment in prayer. Let us pray to those who feel lost, fatherless, alone. Let us pray for all the spiritual orphans out there. Let us pray in the hope that they reach out to God and accept him into their heart. Amen!"

The pastor was truly praying now, giving it his all. He remained on stage, kneeling, his eyes shut tight and hands clasped together, as though trying his best to reach God directly. Others adopted a similar pose as they joined in.

The band returned to the stage and began to play another song, during which about half-a-dozen people approached the front to receive "healing" via the laying on of hands. Tears moistened the eyes of both the healers and those being healed.

I was weirded out by the theatrics of it all, and slightly worried the healers would come for me next; I was in no mood to receive the Holy Spirit. And so, not wanting to stick around, I returned to the foyer for that free cup of coffee.

The barista was a zit-faced teenager with a brown mop of greasy hair who oozed the awkwardness of adolescence and the reluctance of a son forced to engage in voluntary work to make his mother happy. He handed me my order—a cappuccino—in a small paper cup. It tasted okay, a little on the burnt side, but better than instant. Best of all, it gave me something to hold while I stood there in the foyer trying to look natural.

As a single man used to attending public events alone, I've learned to do what I can to not come across as a creep. A lot of single men face this problem. One solution, I've discovered, is to make yourself look busy by holding something—a smart phone, a cup of coffee, a pen. Anything really. Just not your dick.

I was soon approached by a woman in her fifties wearing pink, horn-rimmed glasses and glass bead earrings that perpetually swayed. In a distinctly American accent, she introduced herself as Barbara. Her mood was one of warmth and I detected a genuine desire on her part to make me feel at home.

"I don't recall seeing you before," she said. "I presume it's your first visit?"

"It is," I replied.

"How wonderful! You'll find we're very friendly and welcoming here. Our church is all about community. Some of the younger people can be a bit distant—it's a generational thing, I suppose—but you'll find most of us older folks very approachable."

For a while we engaged in small talk. She was a retired nurse, she said, and happily married. Her husband, Frank, I would meet later. Once I was feeling comfortable and had let down my guard, she got down to brass tacks: was I—like her—a true believer?

"I'm exploring Christianity," I explained. "I suppose you could say I've been searching lately. Since I'm no longer young, I thought it was time to put Christianity to the test."

I detected in her expression a hint of disappointment. Yet there was something else as well—a zeal borne of a hunger to convert me. The woman was on a mission, and to be honest it disturbed me a little.

"I'm sure God brought you here for a reason. He always has a plan. Like yourself, I was always a seeker. But my notion of God was more in line with New Age thought—I referred to God as 'the universe,' that sort of thing. Then, eight years ago, I had a vision while recovering from a hip operation. It was Jesus. I had no particular interest in Jesus at the time, yet he appeared. Two weeks later, I found myself at church."

I was tempted to ask about the operation. A mundane explanation presented itself: that Barbara's so-called vision of Jesus had been an anaesthesia-induced hallucination. These thoughts, however, I wisely kept to myself.

"There's a reason God brought you here," she repeated, winking. "He has a plan for you. I'm sure of it."

2

THE TRAFFIC WAS UNUSUALLY busy for a Sunday morning, and days of unending rain had rendered the roads slippery. I drove with extra caution, gripping the wheel a little tighter than usual, taking each bend nice and slow. As a younger man, I hadn't always driven this carefully. Road safety wasn't something I'd thought about much. Death hardly at all. Now that I was approaching forty, however, barely a day seemed to pass where I didn't contemplate my mortality or consider the possibility of some horrible accident.

Pushing these morbid thoughts aside, I reflected on the pastor's sermon. He'd conveyed his message with eloquence, and his words had left an emotional impact. Is that all it had been, though? An emotional experience? Was there any substance to what he'd said?

Equating God with some kind of father figure struck me as distasteful, even cringeworthy. It conjured an image in my mind of an old bearded man seated on a throne, surrounded by angels playing harps. In fact, as far as I could tell, this very simplistic image of God appealed to most Christians. And no wonder the appeal: psychologically it's comforting to believe that God watches over us, that he loves us the way that a father would love his son or daughter.

Was I a good father, I wondered? My son was only four and already he had to deal with the fact that his parents were separated, spending very little time with me because his mother had been awarded full custody. Not the best start in life for a young lad. I didn't feel like a good father. I felt inadequate, guilty. Yet I also felt there was nothing I could do to fix the situation.

His mother and I were divorced. While together, our relationship had been one of unending conflict. We'd been incompatible, chalk and cheese. We hadn't seen eye to eye on anything, including religion. She was a Christian. I wasn't. She'd wanted to go to church. I'd refused.

Why, then, was I going to church now? Was I trying to prove something to my ex-wife?

Having reached my destination, I parked out the front. Using the rear-view mirror, I took one last glance at my face, paying particular attention to my teeth to make sure there wasn't any food stuck between them. There wasn't: good.

It's not that I wanted to look good for my ex-wife. It's that I didn't want to look like a bum. She'd already decided I was a loser, so why make a mistake that would end up reinforcing her very low opinion of me?

I approached the house. Knocked. Waited. Seconds later my son came tumbling out the door, shouting "Daddy, Daddy." He ran into my arms and I held him tight.

My ex-wife remained standing in the doorway, her expression a scowl of disapproval; she detested witnessing my son's obvious affection for me. "Bring him back at five," she demanded. "And don't be late this time."

In spite of the rain, I drove my son to a park adjacent to the beach. We sat together in the back seat as I read him *The Cat in the Hat*, the car windows foggy with condensation. The moment the weather had cleared, we exited the car and played outside. I pushed him on the swing. We engaged in an imaginary sword fight with sticks. He spent a long time chasing plovers and seagulls but of course never managed to catch a single bird. By the late afternoon he was exhausted, first becoming grumpy, then falling asleep.

I did precisely as his mother requested—I dropped him off at five. Right on the dot.

3

ONCE HOME, I MADE myself a cup of tea and collapsed in a chair in the lounge room, switching on the news to distract myself. I still had beer in the fridge from when I'd been dating Lucy, but I knew that to drink now, while emotions were still raw, was a terrible idea. I'm a sentimental drunk, not a happy drunk. Alcohol does nothing to help me forget my pain. All it does it give me a hangover in the morning and a bad case of the runs.

No thanks, I decided, I'll stick with the tea. I took a sip and sighed loudly. I felt empty, drained, disillusioned. I'd spent the day doing wholesome activities—attending Church, seeing my son—activities that ought to elicit happiness and meaning. Instead I felt emptier, less happy. But why?

Maybe I'm hungry, I thought. Very often the solution to feeling better is as simple as eating a decent meal or getting a proper night's rest. Lately I'd been neglecting both my sleep and my diet.

I stood up and went into the kitchen. Searching the cupboard, I found a small can of *John West* tuna and a packet of instant macaroni and cheese. The latter I cooked in a saucepan on the stove, stirring it with a wooden spoon as I watched the sauce bubble and thicken. Once ready, I spooned it into a bowl, dumping the can of tuna on top and added extra cheese.

Hardly the healthiest meal, but it tasted okay. And what is food anyway but fuel for the body? Besides, I thought, I'm single and male. Single men are easy to please. Single men don't give a shit. What's more, nobody gives a shit about single men. If I died of malnutrition in my apartment, would anyone think to look for me? How long till they found my decaying corpse? A fortnight? A month? Three months?

I continued watching the news while I ate. It was the usual assortment of bullshit: riots in America, protests in Australia; stuff about the pandemic and further lockdowns; stuff about climate change and carbon offsets.

The news was followed by a current affairs program concerning Australia's "domestic violence epidemic." The main "expert" featured on the program was a fat, short-haired, heavily tattooed mum and feminist author, who said we need to teach our sons to express their emotions, be more sensitive, and not follow traditional gender roles. This, she claimed, would help eradicate the problem of "toxic masculinity" and thus violence against women—a problem that, according to her, "all men" are complicit in.

Bullshit, lady! I thought. It's a small minority of men who are responsible for acts of violence against women. Not all men. Here I am, alone in my apartment, minding my own damn business, consuming mac and cheese and shit out of a can, and you're trying to tell me I'm part of the problem!

I needed something to soothe me, to help me calm down. Since I'd already decided that alcohol was a poor choice, I was left with no other options but one: to jerk off. A porn-induced orgasm, though hardly as satisfying as the real thing, was a glorious release, and best of all it was simple and free. Feeling an appetite for something kinky, I typed "dominant woman" into the search bar on *Pornhub*.

I kept scrolling till I found a clip that looked promising. It featured a muscular, black dominatrix with a bulbous ass and huge tits. She was naked except for a pair of shiny, lace-up boots. She stood brandishing a whip while nearby, laid out on his back on what looked like an operating table, moaned and writhed a white guy in a gimp mask, his fat erection pointing in the air like the turret of a tank.

She leaned forward and began gently teasing the tip of his cock with her tongue. She wrapped her fat lips around the full length of his shaft and for a moment it looked as though she was going to blow the guy. Suddenly, with a look of mock disdain, she spat out his cock and laughed.

"Please, mistress," begged the slave. "More! More!"

"Quiet, little man," she retorted. "I make the rules, and if you're lucky and behave you'll get my pussy!"

I was expecting her to straddle and ride him. Or at least get him to eat her out. She didn't though. Or maybe she did. You see, I never got that far through the clip. The moment she blew a loud, rumbling fart in his face and started filling up his mouth with thick, bright-yellow piss, I switched it off, disgusted. I hadn't come. But at least it had solved the problem of my erection.

Was there nothing good these days, I wondered? Even porn was getting worse. What kind of sickos watch fart and piss porn? Why not just regular dominatrix stuff?

That night I tossed and turned, unable to sleep. Despite the cold weather, I felt unusually warm. When sleep finally arrived, I was plagued by strange dreams. In one of my dreams a billy goat came to visit. Its coat was a mix of caramel and white, and its eyes glinted like two yellow marbles. Whenever I tried to move around the apartment, it would appear and block my path, its head titled forward, horns raised, ready to charge.

4

IT WAS A SATURDAY morning, and for the first time in my life I decided to visit the gym. The membership form I'd completed online, using my credit card details for payment. Though expensive, I wasn't too worried about the monthly fees. I could afford it. And besides, in the words of my condescending and successful older brother, Charles, "You can't put a price on your health, bro. You need to get out there. Get healthy. Find a girlfriend. Maybe marry again. It's not too late to fix your life."

I'm not a physically active guy, never have been. In high school, I was the kid who was conveniently sick during just about every sports carnival. This isn't to say I'm lazy. I enjoy a good walk around the block and I'm not afraid to work with my hands, but lifting weights in a gym is not something that comes naturally to me. It was therefore with a sense of reluctance that I attended my first gym session.

Aware that both for practical purposes and to fit in, I ought to wear something "gymy," I donned a pair of light blue shorts, a grey short-sleeve t-shirt, and a pair of sneakers. I looked okay, although the shirt was a little tight, augmenting my paunch, and since I'm not the kind of guy who spends a lot of time in the sun, my hairy, white legs stood out, contrasting with my tanned face and arms.

Upon first entering the gym, I was immediately overwhelmed by the very loud dance music—high energy tunes with lots of bass yet entirely lacking in melody and completely devoid of intelligent lyrics. The smell of perspiring bodies wasn't particularly agreeable either, but this at least I could understand; we're animals and we sweat. It can't be helped.

I was surprised by the shortage of clientele. I counted four in total—three men and one woman. The woman, a chestnut-haired beauty in her mid-twenties, had on a pair of yoga pants so tight that it squeezed her plump ass like a mango wrapped in gladwrap. When she briefly turned in the other direction, I noticed, to my delight, the faintest trace of camel-toe.

Every now and then one of the guys would stare at her, then quickly look away. It soon became apparent to me—though fortunately not to the woman—that I was just as much a perve as the other guys, and for this I felt a little disgusted with myself.

I gingerly approached the desk at reception. After ringing the buzzer, out walked a perfect specimen of masculinity—a muscle bound, blonde-haired dude name Kevin. His white-toothed smile beamed exaggerated positivity, reminding me of an actor from an exercise equipment informercial. He gave me a brief tour of the place, showing me first the cardio equipment, then the weights, followed by the boxing room, and concluded by wishing me the best with my "fitness goals."

With my towel and water bottle tucked under my arm, I headed straight to the machine that struck me as the least intimidating: one of the treadmills. I'd never used a treadmill before, though I quickly got the hang of it, adjusting the speed to that of a brisk walk. Enough of a workout to increase my heart rate and cause me to perspire, but not so exhausting that I couldn't sustain the pace for the duration of the machine's timer—which was currently set to 25 minutes.

I soon became aware of a short, fat, bespectacled man at the other end of the gym, puffing away on the lat pulldown machine. He looked about fifty, maybe older. Physical strain had augmented his already ruddy complexion, such that he resembled a ripe tomato. Perspiration oozed from every pore of his body, rendering the lenses of his glasses heavily fogged. His belly bulged out like a mountain, taking his shirt with it and leaving a large gap at the bottom.

On the leg machine adjacent sat the young woman from earlier. The fat guy had his eyes on her, clearly checking her out. I watched as, to my surprise, he ceased what he was doing and walked over to talk to her. She looked uncomfortable; he was either oblivious to her discomfort or too damn ballsy to care. She's out of his league, I thought, way out of his league, but I admire his bravery for having a go.

They didn't speak for long. On account of the loud music, I managed to catch only a few words, one of which, oddly enough, was "Jesus."

The fat guy seemed pleased by the outcome of the interaction, walking away with a satisfied smile on his face. After wiping down his machine, he took a long drink from his aluminium flask and started in my direction.

"Howdy, cobber," I heard him say as he mounted the treadmill adjacent to mine. He had dark patches of sweat under both arms, twin sources of eye-watering stench. I gave a non-committal hello, suppressing the urge to scrunch up my nose.

He pointed a fat, calloused finger in my direction. Squinting, he said, "I've seen you before. You came to church recently, yes?"

At first I was confused; then it struck me that he looked familiar. "Yes," I admitted, "I was there last week."

He introduced himself as Brian and we shook. His hand felt damp and cold, like an uncooked slab of porterhouse steak. I wiped my palm on the side of my shorts.

As he started up his machine, he began telling me about his life, projecting his words through stained, crooked teeth and lips moist with spittle.

He hadn't always been a Christian, he explained. As a youth he'd been lost and troubled, spending his days chasing women, getting into fights at the pub, and repeatedly disappointing his parents. A pot smoker and heavy drinker, he was unable to hold down a job for more than a couple of weeks.

Once, while working as a vineyard labourer, he had a habit of drinking all night and showing up to work the next day hung-over and tired. During lunch breaks and when the boss wasn't looking, he'd manage to sneak in a brief catnap. This became a problem when, one day, the boss caught him asleep under a tree with the front of his shirt all covered in vomit.

One evening, feeling suicidal, he experienced a sudden and unexpected compulsion to pray to God. He hadn't prayed since he was a child, and the urge to do so now seemed to him divinely inspired, as though God were giving him a chance to turn his life around. No sooner had he closed his eyes when he was overcome by the sound of a mighty, rushing wind—what he took to be the very presence of God.

The experience left him terrified and overwhelmed, but also taught him "respect for the Lord." His state of mind improved after that and so too his life. He stopped "rebelling" against God and began to live in accordance with scripture. He quit drinking, quit smoking marijuana, and started going to church and attending AA.

"How's your relationship with God?" Brian finally asked me.

"It's hard to say," I replied. "So far God hasn't made himself known to me."

"Well, I suggest you pray on it. Pray for guidance. It's the only way. If you pray on it, God will come, believe me, and when he does it'll shake you to your very core."

I nodded, usure what to say.

He let out a laugh. "I realise I tend to come across as... passionate. Can't help it. It's the way God made me."

I tried to return the smile, but it came out crooked, insincere. "The woman you were talking to earlier, any luck getting her to listen to the good news?"

He was silent for a moment, confused; then a look of recognition crossed his face. "Oh, her. Can't say she was receptive, no." He leaned in close and added with a wink, "The good-looking ones are a hard sell."

I stayed on the treadmill for another twenty minutes, until I was breathless and couldn't go on. As I was finishing up, Brian said goodbye and left. He had a busy day ahead of him, he said.

On my way out, I saw Brian talking to a skinny, dark-haired woman in the parking lot. She was dressed to go to the gym, but, due to being waylaid by Brian, hadn't yet made it through the front door.

Hers were the characteristics of a former junkie and one who'd lived rough: hollow cheeks, sunken eyes, poor teeth, little muscle, little fat, combined with an expression of permanent sadness and defeat. Now, it would seem, she was trying to turn her life around, in part by getting fit.

I slipped by without Brian noticing. I was sure he'd have better luck with this one.

5

IMAGINE THERE'S A MAN who's visit every major attraction in his local area except for the most popular and significant one of all. Let's say it's a mountain.

The man keeps bumping into people who rave about the mountain, telling him how majestic and wonderful it is, and how, if he goes, it'll change his life for the better. He resents these comments, because he has his own particular view of things, and nowhere in his mind and in his way of thinking is there a logical place for the mountain to fit. To him it represents something foreign, something incongruous. Simply put, he doesn't like the look of the thing.

As the years pass by, it dawns on the man that if doesn't visit the mountain soon he may lose his opportunity to do so forever. With maturity comes humility and the recognition that he doesn't know as much as he thought he knew. He begins to doubt himself, to question all of his cherished assumptions and beliefs. He begins to wonder if his opinion of the mountain was mistaken all along.

Maybe those people who spoke highly of the mountain were in fact correct? Maybe it's the very thing he's been searching for his entire life? Maybe it's the site of buried treasure? Maybe on the mountain he'll meet the women of his dreams, his soul mate? Or find enlightenment there? Or meet God on its summit?

Christianity was my unexplored mountain. That I had an ex-wife who was Christian, plus an ex-girlfriend who, shortly before our relationship ended, spontaneously converted to Christianity—both of whom regarded me as a sinner in need of the love and mercy of Jesus—further strengthened my resolve to once and for all don my hiking boots, grab my backpack and water bottle, and start climbing.

So that's what I did: I climbed.

6

ATTENDING CHURCH EACH WEEK wasn't easy, but I kept at it, convinced that, somehow, it was doing me good.

My plan was to become—if not an actual Christian—then someone who embodied all the best Christian qualities: good social skills, a strong work ethic, sound morals, a deep appreciation of the importance of community. And maybe, I thought, as a result of acquiring these qualities, I'd finally achieve success.

Success for me included a woman in the picture. Not just any woman, either, but a good Christian woman from a stable family. Not another slut. I was through with dating sluts.

Was I excepting too much of Christianity? Probably. But I didn't let this phase me. I had a plan and I was sticking to it, God willing, if you'll pardon the pun.

Mine was a path towards self-improvement—spiritually, mentally, physically—and already I could feel myself becoming stronger, more organised, more motivated, more alert. I was beginning to like the new me.

My Sunday morning ritual consisted of waking up early, eating a hearty breakfast of bacon and eggs, tidying my apartment, then reading a few passages of the Bible before making the trip to church. I made sure to dress well for the occasion, donning a long-sleeve, button-up shirt, well-fitted trousers and a jacket. I was thorough, paying close attention to each tiny detail. Not once did I neglect to iron my shirt or polish my shoes. If I managed to wake up early enough, I'd hit the gym before doing all of the above, working out for at least half-an-hour.

I soon made friends at church. One Sunday following the sermon, as I sat in the foyer drinking a coffee (no longer free, but paid for), I was approached by a smartly-dressed Asian couple in their mid-to-late-twenties. The guy introduced himself as Peter. His wife, whose English left much to be desired, gave her name as June.

They were from Melbourne, explained Peter, but had moved over for work. He was a podiatrist and she a nurse. When it came time to talk about my own line of work—that of writing books, freelance journalism and the occasional bit of editing—I kept it brief. Mention the word "writer" and people suspect you're a bum and a loser. Reveal you haven't written a best-seller, and they conclude you're precisely that.

"How are you finding life here?" I asked. "Not too boring, I hope, compared to the big city?"

Peter tilted his head as he pondered my question. "At first it was... challenging. There were many adjustments to be made. Now, though, we're happy. It's a wonderful community, and it's beginning to feel like home."

"It's a small place," I replied, "and the locals can be cliquey."

"Ah, well," said Peter, "that's why we believe and trust in God—we know that whatever happens in life, wherever we end up, he has our back."

My response came involuntarily: "Really?"

There was a period of awkward silence; then Peter cleared his throat. "Absolutely. God provides no matter what. He loves each and every one of us. He knows us better than we know ourselves."

"Ever hair on your head," interjected June. "God knows... precise number."

"That's right," agreed Peter. "We're his children. He takes care of us. All God asks in return is that we have faith in him. When we surrender to God, when we hand our lives over to him, we find that we no longer lack for anything."

"If you want something from God, then no problem," said June. "You pray for it. It happen. Always."

"So let me get this straight," I asked, addressing the two of them. "You're saying that God will give you things... if you believe in him and pray for it?"

"Within reason," said Peter, nodding. "I know that God provides because I've experienced it first-hand. If it wasn't for God, I'd have never met June."

With genuine curiosity, I asked, "God brought the two of you together?"

What followed was a cute and romantic story. They first met, explained Peter, several years ago, while living in the same share-house in Melbourne. There were five other tenants besides them, and they just so happened to be the only two Christians in the entire household. How they'd met, according to Peter, couldn't have been a coincidence; it was too improbable.

"So you see," concluded Peter, "God works miracles. He helps us. He brings people together. *If* we allow him to do so."

I was sceptical, of course, but my scepticism didn't come from a place of cynicism or rebellion. It wasn't because I doubted the existence of God per se. It's because I struggled to accept the existence of a God as believed in by Peter, June and other Christians. Theirs was a personal, loving God. A God who answered the prayers of those in need and who ensured that his children were well provided for.

An impersonal God, a kind of "universal intelligence," was something I could theoretically accept. Yet the problem is that, when attempting to conceive of such a being, there was no emotional energy behind it, nothing I could pin down or objectify. It was too vague a concept, too airy-fairy. How does a person relate to that which is impersonal? What, indeed, is the point of trying?

Before leaving church that day, I gave Peter my number and we agreed to catch up one weekend. He wanted to tell me more about God, about the "miracles" that he and June had experienced as Christians, about how, according to them, God was continually blessing their lives.

Whereas, in the past, I had a tendency to dismiss all religious claims, especially those of Christians, I saw no reason to do so now, but rather every reason to keep an open-mind on the off chance I might be wrong. Christianity, I reminded myself, was my unexplored mountain.

To explore a mountain, you don't simply gaze at the thing from afar and complain about how steep it is. You have to climb it.

7

— · —

WHEN I TOOK MY son to the park that afternoon, he was grumpy, miserable, tired. Nothing seemed to make him happy. Yet I persisted in my fatherly efforts to ensure that the outing wasn't a complete waste of time.

First we tried the swing. After three pushes, he got upset, started crying. While I had my back turned, he squirmed out of his seat and ran off down the hill. I managed to catch up to him and grab him right before he reached the edge of the road.

Next we tried the playground with the slide and climbers. He'd go up a few rungs, get discouraged, then immediately hop down. As for the slide, he wanted to crawl up it, rather than slide down it. This caused problems for the other children. Disaster struck when a blonde-haired girl of about eight bumped into my son as she was coming down and he going up. The impact resulted in two crying children.

The girl's father, a tall, bearded guy in his 40s dressed in a *Nirvana* t-shirt and skinny jeans, witnessed the incident from the barbeque area—where he'd been cooking sausages and steaks—and immediately came running over.

"Sorry," I offered. "My son can be a bit clumsy sometimes, but he means well."

"Maybe you should keep a closer eye on your son," he responded, glowering. He picked up his daughter, held her in his arms.

Glancing over at the barbeque area, I noticed several pairs of hostile eyes pointed in my direction. They belonged to the girl's mother, a woman with pink hair and tattoos across both arms, along with the girl's two brothers, both in their early-teens.

"I was watching him the whole time," I told the father. "As I said, it was an accident."

"Mate, I don't give a shit. You've ruined my daughter's birthday. And I bet the food's burnt now too, so thanks for that."

I watched the guy storm off, still holding his daughter.

Anger rose inside of me, but I wisely held my tongue, resisting the urge to call the guy a "miserable fuck." I immediately took my son and headed to the car. Time to leave, I decided. Either that or run the risk of completely losing my cool.

My son fell asleep as we were driving down the highway, his little head slumped against the padding of his car seat.

For a while I drove around aimlessly, not sure where to go, before settling on the beach as my best option. I found a quiet, private spot that offered a panoramic view of crashing waves and expansive sky. I parked, turned off the ignition.

With the window cracked open and my seat reclined, I sat with eyes closed, relaxing and soaking up the warmth of the sun.

Just as I was on the verge of drifting off to sleep, I felt my phone vibrate in my pocket. It was Peter.

There must have been a hint of lethargy in my voice, because immediately he asked, "I hope I haven't caught you at a bad time, Chuck?"

"Not at all," I answered, adjusting the seat to its upright position. I quickly checked the backseat—my son was still asleep. What a relief.

"The reason for my call is that June and I are having a special dinner on Wednesday night. We'd like to know if you'd care to join us."

I'm not a fan of dinner parties. Eating in the presence of others while simultaneously engaging in small talk is not something I particularly enjoy.

"Wednesday, eh? I'm not sure if I can make it," I lied. "There's a chance I'll be busy that night."

"Ah, that's a shame. There's a specific reason we'd like you to join us."

"Oh."

"It was actually June's idea. This may sound a bit strange to someone who's still fairly new to Christianity, but a small number of us at church are sensitive to the ways of the Holy Spirit. This can take the form of prophecies, intuitions, advice. Of course, I don't have this ability myself. June does though, and she's very accurate."

"You're saying that June receives... messages from God?"

"Well, yes. And in this case the Spirit told her there's someone you ought to meet. She's a friend of ours. Her name's Stephanie."

It took me a few seconds to comprehend the implication behind Peter's words. "You mean, like, a blind date?"

He laughed. "When God's involved, it's never blind, but if that's what you want to call it, then yes."

The decision was easy to make. I'd never been on a blind date before, and while I knew the experience would undoubtedly be nerve-racking, the opportunity to meet a woman was not something I could easily pass up. Maybe God had my back after all. Perhaps my days of singledom would soon be over.

"You know what, Wednesday night should be fine," I said. "I'll be there."

8

I KEPT BUMPING INTO Brian at the gym. It's as though our lives were synchronised. I'd arrive early, head straight to the treadmill, and within ten minutes he'd saunter through the front door, towel under his arm, ready for his workout. Always eager to chat, he'd insist on using the treadmill directly adjacent to mine. At first, I could barely tolerate his presence. Over time I came to like the guy enough to endure his annoying habits and long sermons.

One morning, in an attempt to steer the topic away from Christianity, I asked him about his health and fitness goals and whether he was pleased with his progress.

"I feel great," he replied, flashing a beaming smile. "Though you wouldn't know it by looking at me, I'm shedding the pounds."

I gave him a thumbs up. "Well done."

"Thanks. It's a battle though. I like food. Actually, I *love* food."

"Don't we all," I replied.

"Ha! You don't strike me as the kind of guy who struggles with gluttony, Chuck." He looked me up and down. "You're a good-looking bloke. Slim. Healthy skin. Nice muscle tone. I'm surprised you bother coming to the gym."

The homosexual undertones of the remark weren't lost on me. I felt self-conscious, uncomfortable. "I'm not as healthy as I look," I said. "I lose my breath quickly. And my belly is larger than it should be."

He laughed, slapping his belly with the palm of his hand. It wobbled like a bowl of gelatine dessert. "*This* is what you call a belly. Yours is nothing. When I look down, I can't even find my dick!"

I laughed. Brian could be funny sometimes. Especially when making fun of himself.

"I want to be able to look down," he added, "and actually see something. Not this mountain of blubber."

"Keep shedding the pounds and I'm sure you'll get there eventually," I replied.

We were both silent for a moment. Bobbing up and down on the elliptical machine in front of us was a woman in her thirties wearing light-green leggings and a white crop top. Her face was plain, but her physique was something to behold. I noticed Brian ogling her plump booty with greater eagerness than I.

He turned and looked at me. "Do you have a woman in your life?"

"No. Divorced. You?"

"Also divorced. Marie and I separated five years ago. We're still good friends though. I haven't given up hope that one day we'll be reunited."

For a moment Brian looked like a sad little boy and I couldn't help but feel sorry for him. Trying to uplift his mood, I said, "It's nice to know there's a chance you'll get back together again."

"Yes. Mind you, it's unlikely to happen in this lifetime."

I was confused. Was he referring to reincarnation? Surely not. The confusion must have registered on my face, because a moment later he spoke again. "God works miracles, Chuck. He heals broken relationships, brings people together again. Husbands and wives. Brothers and sisters. Long lost friends. I've seen it happen within the church community. And if it doesn't happen in this lifetime, it happens in the next—in heaven."

I now understood what he meant. He meant he'd be reunited with his ex-wife in heaven, made husband and wife again.

"You must really love the woman," I said, "to want to be with her for all eternity."

He nodded. "Marriage is sacred. Not something to be trifled with. It's an eternal bond."

"So why did you and Marie divorce in the first place then?"

He sighed. "It wasn't my idea. Marie pushed for it. She met someone else. Although that relationship didn't last and since then she's been single."

"Oh. Yet you're still good friends?"

"Let's just say she puts up with me," he laughed. "We get along well enough to be there for Gemma. We don't sleep or live together—there's no intimacy, and she gets annoyed if I visit too often —but at least I know I'm doing my part to ensure that Gemma gets taken care of."

"Gemma is your daughter?"

"Well, technically I'm not the father. I suppose you could say I'm the stepfather. Gemma has no contact with her biological father, and very little contact with Marie. Marie finds the situation too stressful. I'm the main carer. When Gemma isn't with me, she lives in a care home."

It took me a moment to realise that I'd seen Gemma at church accompanied by Brian. She was a tall, stocky girl, about fifteen-years-old. Wore earmuffs and a heavy woollen sweater. Her features were typical of someone with down syndrome: slanted eyes, a small chin, the face round and moon-like. I had initially assumed she was Chinese; she was actually half-Māori on her mother's side.

Each week at church Gemma stood at the very front, as close to the stage as she could possibly get in order to enhance her enjoyment of the music. She was non-verbal, couldn't speak a single word of English, so communicated via basic sign language. When excited or agitated, she'd call out loudly, emitting a noise that sounded like an animal in pain. The parishioners had learned to ignore the sounds, although some welcomed them, convinced that Gemma was responding to the presence of the Holy Spirit.

I asked Brian, "What made you decided to look after Gemma, even though she isn't technically your daughter and even though you and Marie are separated?"

He regarded me with an expression of pity, as though the answer to my question were obvious, so obvious as to suggest some mental or spiritual deficiency on my part. "It's love, Chuck. I'm doing it because of love."

9

I WAS LIVING, AS I said, in a crumby apartment. Had been since my divorce. It was the cheapest place I could find at the time. Perfect for a freelance journalist and author on a limited budget. Cheap things, though, come with a price of their own.

My apartment was located above a warehouse that previously functioned as a print shop, and prior to that, a tyre shop. It was originally an office that had since been converted into a living space, albeit poorly.

The kitchen, for example, lacked an extractor fan. Consequently, whenever I cooked dinner on the stove, the cooking fumes and steam would accumulate in the kitchen, building into a giant cloud that would trigger the smoke alarm before settling on the walls and ceiling. One girlfriend noted with a lack of humour that my apartment was constantly "moist."

That the building was without insulation, save for a thin coating of plaster on the reinforced concrete walls and ceiling, further contributed to the build-up of moisture. After one or more days of little sunshine, the interior surfaces would remain as cold as ice, attracting condensation like a nylon tent.

It became a morning ritual of mine to gaze up from my bed at the ceiling and count the hanging droplets. Occasionally one would come loose, landing with a splash in my eye or on my cheek. Hardly a great way to start the day. These icy droplets I dubbed "the devil's piss."

Moisture, of course, attracts mould. They'd sprout on the ceiling like some alien parasite; lifeforms thick, black and hungry. I'd remove a patch of mould with bleach, only to discover a week later that it had either grown back or that a new patch had appeared somewhere else. I must've breathed in a lot of mould spores. I'm sure it damaged my health in a permanent way.

Yet the apartment was not without its positive features. The bathroom was tiny, barely a few square meters, but somehow, for some reason, the owner had installed a big old tub—a steel, enamel-coated monstrosity speckled with rust and paint stains.

I didn't make use of the tub very often. When I did, however, I'd go all out, bathing in the manner of a king. I'd fill the tub almost to the brim, adding plenty of hot. Sometimes I'd throw in a bath bomb or two. Lying fully immersed in the water except for my face, I'd close my eyes, relax, and temporarily forget about my crappy life and all of my problems: my worries, my loneliness, my divorce, my burdens, my obstacles and limitations.

One rainy afternoon, I decided to draw a bath not to relax and forget but to relax—and hopefully —awaken. It was time, I decided, to take stock of my life, time to figure out how to move ahead, how to improve, how to better myself. Instead of running away from my problems, I would confront them head on. Tub-style.

A strange idea, I admit, yet there was a certain method to my madness. I'd read somewhere that deep relaxation promotes the free expression of the subconscious, and what better way to relax than by means of a hot bath? By getting in touch with my subconscious, by exposing its depths, the answers I so badly sought would reveal themselves. Or so I hoped.

As I settled into the water with a wet rag over my face, I imagined my life as a movie and myself the protagonist. The intention behind this was to create distance between myself and my problems, giving my thoughts free expression and allowing the emergence of creative ideas and solutions.

My protagonist, I knew, was in a less than enviable situation. He was single, divorced. The divorce hadn't resulted in a clean break either. There was a child involved, a little boy, which meant the protagonist and his ex-wife were forever shackled to one another.

Or were they? He had a choice. He could run away, renounce his responsibility as a father, make a new life for himself somewhere else. He could become what society called a "deadbeat dad." Or— and this he'd already chosen to do—he could remain, try to be a part of his son's life, learn to put up with his ex-wife's toxic behaviour, bad moods and unreasonable demands.

My protagonist's main goal was to rebuild his life, to turn it around for the better. This would require strength, bravery and commitment, along with community support and the love of a good woman. In time, if he managed to stay true to his course, he would emerge victorious, as a man reinvented and reborn.

Since my protagonist was no longer young, time was of the essence. Each day he would need to remind himself that the clock was ticking and each day he would need to work hard. He could no longer afford to be lazy, complacent, to expect things to work out on their own. Blaming others was not an option. Only he was responsible for both his successes and failures.

I sat up in the bath, removed the rag from my face and worked the trapped water out of my ears by cupping my palms over them. The message was clear: I needed to keep going to church, to continue climbing my unexplored mountain. Already I was making progress. Already I had a date lined up. Surely this was a sign I was on the right path?

When I noticed the water becoming cloudy, tepid, and my skin wrinkled, I took this as an indication that it was time to climb out. Once dry and dressed, I felt not exactly reborn, but clean.

10

—·—

FOR SOME REASON BARBARA and Frank took a special interest in me. Whereas Barbara was a regular church attendee, Frank—on account of his advanced age and tentative health—attended church only once a month on average. A tall, bald-headed guy in his sixties with a tan complexion and dark eyes, he moved with the assurance and precision of a reptile. On his head sat a brown fiddler cap, and around his wrinkled neck dangled a thick, wooden cross. He looked out of place in Tasmania, with its high precipitation and abundance of greenery. I imagined him at home in some desert somewhere, among red soil, cacti and wide-open skies.

One afternoon they invited me over for coffee. Their home, perched on the top of a steep hill, afforded a spectacular view of the ocean. It was their yard, however, that most absorbed my attention. Neat and well-maintained, it featured rose bushes, fruit trees, small hedges, and a bright green lawn that had been trimmed to perfection.

There were garden gnomes aplenty—some perched on the grass, others hidden among shrubs. While most were bearded men in pointy hats brandishing shovels and other implements, there were others of a more eccentric nature: one dressed in full biker gear, another smoking a pipe, several dressed as soldiers armed with machine guns, and at least a couple that were naked, one of them a female with large breasts.

We sat outside on the deck on cane chairs, drinking tea from decorative cups. On the glass-top table in front of us sat bowls of fruit and biscuits, along with a bag of fresh doughnuts I'd brought along for the occasion.

The table was not without a gnome of its own. Propped up on a little platform like some kind of deity, this particular character had his pants pulled down and his ass in the air, mooning onlookers. So incongruous was its presence that, initially, it left me at a complete loss of words.

"You have a beautiful house," I said. "Amazing view of the ocean from here."

"Thank you," replied Frank. "Barbara and I have a special relationship with the ocean."

They looked at each other knowingly; then Barbara said, "Before this we lived on a sailing boat. Sailed around Asia. The pacific. Quite an adventurous life. Eventually we decided it was time to put down roots."

Frank took a sip of tea, cleared his throat. "Mind you, we still have plenty of adventures, even though my health isn't quite what it used to be." He turned to Barbara. "Wouldn't you agree, dear?"

She nodded, smiling. The smile looked unconvincing.

Barbara was younger than Frank by a good twenty years. The age difference intrigued me, but I didn't dare ask about it.

Frank proved to be an excellent storyteller, his speech eloquent, measured and rich with emotion. What followed was a detailed account of his life and how he'd come to find Jesus.

He grew up in a poor and highly dysfunctional home, his father alcoholic and his mother bipolar. In his early twenties he started using drugs as an escape: first marijuana, then cocaine and speed, and finally heroin.

These addictions destabilised his life and set him on a path of self-destruction. His marriage fell apart, then his business as a handyman. He was denied access to his children. Unemployed and broke, he was forced to borrow money from his brother to help pay his child support bills.

Early one morning he decided to end his own life. He got up, showered, dressed, had breakfast, then spent the next hour penning farewell letters to friends and family members. He had a plan: after posting the letters at the nearby post office, he would take the exit to the highway; along the side of the highway grew many tall pines; he would choose one that was strong and sturdy and, with the accelerator pedal pressed to the floor, aim straight for it. Death by intentional car crash.

He was about to reach for his car keys and head out the door when a voice appeared in his head, causing him to stop and pause. It sounded like a wise, elderly male. Quoting the Bible, it said, "Why should you die before your time?"

He felt that the voice was that of an angel, if not God himself. A feeling of peace and love overcame him and he fell to the floor crying tears of sadness and joy. He returned the keys to the mantle, went back to bed, and had one of the best sleeps of his life.

The following day he checked himself into a rehab clinic, where he spent the next few months getting clean and studying the Bible. So profound an effect did the words of the Good Book have on him—this in combination with the voice that saved his life—that he decided to "submit to Jesus." Almost instantly, the urge to touch drugs and alcohol vanished and he found himself "reborn anew."

"My rebirth through Jesus and the Holy Spirit was similar," observed Barbara. "When I accepted Jesus into my heart, it transformed me. It's as though a heavy weight was lifted from my soul."

"You mean you now feel unburdened?" I asked.

I'd heard other Christians talk about their conversion in similar terms. With Jesus guiding and protecting them, they felt lighter, no longer weighed down by the world. I was curious to know more about this feeling. It was something, I suppose, that I wanted to experience myself.

"Completely unburdened," Barbara replied, smiling and stretching out her arms to the sky.

"What's it like to feel that way?"

It was Frank who answered my question, though not directly. "One time Barbara and I were sailing around Thailand, between the islands of Phuket and Ko Phi Phi. The water there is a beautiful turquoise blue, almost transparent. We were passing through a narrow channel. I assumed there was plenty of clearance between the bottom of the hull and the seabed. I was mistaken. I'd failed to notice a shoal right in front of us. We were headed straight for it, and by that stage it was too late to change course."

Barbara took up the story. "Then a miracle happened. We were standing there on the deck bracing ourselves for impact. All of a sudden, virtually out of nowhere, a wave rose up behind us. It picked up the yacht like a giant hand and carried us over the shoal to safety."

"Had that wave not appeared at that precise moment... well... I hate to think," said Frank. "We would have run aground. As for the yacht—damaged beyond repair."

"And you think it was the work of God?" I asked.

"I do," he replied. "But there's another reason I mention this story. It's to illustrate a point. God is vast and powerful like the ocean. We convince ourselves that God doesn't exist, and so, instead of trusting the ocean, instead of allowing it to carry us to safety, we grab the tiller firmly and try to manipulate the boat. This is one of Satan's greatest deceptions: that we're all alone, that there's no God, that it's us against the world, against nature, against the ocean."

I was quiet for a moment as I contemplated Frank's story, my eyes fixed on the distant ocean, the waves choppy and tipped with white foam. It looked both beautiful and hostile.

Frank spoke again: "I can tell what it is that you yearn for, Chuck. Part of you wants to give yourself to God, but there's another part of you that's resisting. Trust me, life is so much better when you simply… surrender."

"He's right," said Barbara. "There's no comparison between how I'm living now and how I was living before."

"I'm sure it's comforting to let go and allow a higher power to do the steering," I said. "Navigating your own boat isn't easy. The fact is, not once in my life have I experienced a miracle from God. He's never helped me—assuming he exists at all. I've had to go it alone. There's tremendous risk here, see? If I surrender and allow myself to fully accept God, and if He then fails to deliver on his promises, the disappointment will be too much to bear. It would be absolutely crushing. Know what I mean?"

The words had come tumbling out of my mouth. I'd been thinking out loud as much as voicing my opinion. I studied Frank and Barbara's faces, worried I may have said too much and perhaps disappointed them. There was no indication that I had.

"We need to pray," said Barbara, giving me a reassuring pat on the knee.

I didn't want to pray, but I did the polite thing— I closed my eyes and pretended to participate.

"Dear Lord," began Barbara, "we thank you for bringing the three of us together on this very fine day. We ask, Lord, that you bless this young man in our company. Bless him and guide him towards your light, Lord, and help open his eyes to your glory, benevolence and majesty. Amen."

"Thanks for that," I said, feeling embarrassed. Eager to change the topic, I pointed to the mooning gnome sat atop the table. "What's the story behind this, er, interesting character?"

Smiling in delight, Barbara said, "That interesting character is named Gerald."

"Gerald, okay. I assume he's your favourite gnome?"

"Not only is Gerald our favourite, we consider him a part of the family," said Frank.

I couldn't tell if Frank was being facetious. I studied his face for a smile or a wink but neither appeared.

"Does he have some kind of religious significance?" I asked.

"I suppose he does," said Barbara. "You'll notice that Gerald is bearing his backside. He's quite a naughty boy. You're a naughty boy, aren't you, Gerald?"

Watching Barbara talk to a gnome was both surreal and disconcerting.

"I think what Barbara's trying to express," said Frank, "is that God has a way of revealing himself in even the smallest things. Whether it be in a beautiful painting. A tree. A droplet of water. Or..."

"—a garden gnome," I cut in.

"Or a garden gnome," echoed Frank.

Feeling the urge to empty my bladder, I asked where the bathroom was and Frank gave me directions.

I excused myself and entered the house. The bathroom was located down the end of the hall, past two bedrooms and a study. I closed the door, locked it. I flipped up the lid and let loose, sighing with relief as I watched the piss hit the side of the bowl and steam rise.

Finished, I turned on the spigot to wash my hands. There was no soap. I figured there must be some soap somewhere, either in the cabinet above the sink or in one of the draws below. I checked both, still no soap. What I did find, however, was a large bottle of water-based lube and a 50mg box of Viagra tablets.

Exasperated, I drew back the curtain that hung in front of the bath. Surely here I'd find some soap, I thought. I was in luck. Perched on the edge of the tub was a small sliver of soap, just enough to wash my hands with. I found something else, too —something so bizarre that, to this day, I still wonder if it wasn't a product of my imagination.

It sat on a shelf above the far end of the bath, adjacent to a decorative plastic fern. It was an elderly male gnome fucking a young female gnome from behind, doggystyle. While the male gnome was clearly enjoying the act, the expression on his face one of pure, ferocious lust, the female gnome, whose dress had been raised above her ass and underwear pulled aside, looked terrified and violated, as though she were being raped.

I'm no prude. Normally I'd laugh at two gnomes fucking. In this case, I was unable to find any humour in the thing. It looked wrong. Not just wrong, but sinister, spooky.

When I came back outside, Frank and Barbara hadn't moved from their chairs. Frank had a copy of the Bible on his lap and was thumbing through it, smiling to himself contentedly. Barbara was engaged in a telephone call with a customer service representative at her bank.

I made an excuse and left. Three weeks later I was invited back. I declined.

11

‒‒·‒

WHY THE INCESSANT SEARCH for truth? Why couldn't I settle for a normal life and simply be happy?

I was only four when my parents separated and my mother moved out of the house. A hippy, feminist and aspiring Buddhist, she longed for peace, freedom, and the opportunity to become enlightened. Children she saw as an obstacle to happiness. She figured that my father, an angst-ridden writer and former musician with a history of alcoholism, would be able to figure it out on his own. And if he didn't? Well, so be it.

I stood outside bawling as I watched my mother drive off in her white Hillman Minx, convinced I'd never see her again, that she no longer loved me. Emotion continued to roll out of me in waves until, spent from the sheer exhaustion of it all, I collapsed on the ground like a rag doll, my tears, spit and snot combining with the dirt beneath me to create a muddy mess.

The chronic bed wetting started soon after. My pyjamas all wet with piss in the morning. A big, wet patch in the middle of the mattress. The stench of ammonia so powerful it made my eyes sting. You can throw the bedding in the washing machine, sure, air out the mattress too, but the smell will linger and the stains will remain.

"You're a piss-pot," my brother would taunt.

"You're being mean," I'd say.

"So what? You're just a baby. And dad loves me more than you."

He was right: he was dad's favourite. The golden boy. My dad had an endearing nickname for him, but not one for me. Now and then I wondered if my dad loved me at all.

Once custody issues were settled, my brother and I started visiting our mother every fortnight. She lived an hour's drive away, over the other side of the mountain, on a block of land she owned communally with a bunch of other hippies and alternative freaks.

Its residents included twin boys who were half-Japanese, on their father's side. Even more unique, they had two mums; both fat and Caucasian, both with permanently joyless expressions. The boys weren't much fun to play with. They were sad and cried all the time because they missed their dad.

Their dad I only saw once. He was shy and spoke little English. No match for the two angry lesbians, he returned to Japan, I'm told, where he died shortly after from leukemia.

Then there was the guy we called Jesus. He had the messiah look down pat: long hair and beard, leather sandals, white flowing robe down to his ankles. To his credit, he had better hygiene than the other hippies. He smelt of patchouli, combed and oiled his hair to perfection, kept his feet well-pedicured and always made sure to remove his footwear before stepping inside. The guy was as delicate as a flower, more feminine than masculine.

I have an image of Jesus and my mother dancing together in the middle of the loungeroom to the tunes of *Fleetwood Mac*; hips swaying and arms waving, a cloud of pot smoke surrounding them. They dated for a while, but it didn't work out. My mother was an introvert, Jesus more so. You can't sustain a relationship when there's no conversation.

There was also a guy who spent a lot of time up trees, an ability he'd perfected for the express purpose of disrupting the local logging industry. We called him Possum. His hygiene left much to be desired; he rarely if ever showered. He was tall, skinny, and got around without shoes. So calloused and off-colour were his feet that they resembled slabs of parmesan cheese. His toenails he kept purposely long and thick so as to enhance his grip when climbing trees.

The top half of the man—or, perhaps more accurately, creature—was no less hideous. Years of neglecting to brush, wash and cut his hair had given rise to filthy dreadlocks, of which he was extremely proud. He had a gaunt face and cruel eyes. Not one person liked the guy—he was an unabashed asshole—though few could deny that he lived up to his nickname: he could scale a blue gum in a matter of minutes.

Though there existed a community centre where the hippies would gather for the occasional meeting or group dinner, each member of the community (or family) had their own separate dwelling, some little more than poorly constructed shacks, others actual houses fitted with all the modern amenities. Each dwelling, fortunately, was a good distance apart from those adjacent, and mostly people kept to themselves and respected each other's privacy.

For a while my mother lived in an octagonal-shaped house we referred to as "the studio." It was built out of granite rock and mortar. Six of its sides had large windows, providing impressive views and letting in plenty of light. The interior was open plan, although lengths of cloth had been hung from the ceiling to create some measure of privacy.

A roaring wood fire kept the place warm throughout the cooler months. There was a kitchenette with a sink, though no running water; water for drinking and washing we collected in buckets from a nearby creek. Baths we took outside in a round tin tub, first heating the water in saucepans on the stove.

These outdoor baths were mostly pleasant, at least until the water grew tepid. As a kid I had no issue being naked in front of family members, my ding-a-ling on full display. Pissing I developed into an artform; I loved seeing how far I could piss, and if I managed to drown an ant or two in the process, I felt mighty, like a god. Taking a dump, on the other hand, was a horrible ordeal.

The toilet consisted of an open hole over which you had to squat. Once done, you'd throw in a few handfuls of sawdust. This helped to hide all those squirming brown turds. Shit, though, is shit. It smells to high heaven and it attracts flies and maggots.

———

My mother's best friends were a Buddhist couple named Jennifer and Arnold. Originally from England, they'd immigrated to Australian during the early '80s to pursue an alternative lifestyle, constructing a house deep in the forest out of timber they'd salvaged from the tip. It was due to their influence, at least in part, that my mother became a Buddhist.

Every now and then they'd host a party at their house in which they and their guests would get stoned and drunk and dance all night to the music of Bob Dylan, the *Grateful Dead* and Neil Young. A bit like Woodstock, but on a far smaller scale, featuring hippies past their prime.

My mother didn't miss a single one of these parties, bringing us children along. Sometimes we'd stay the entire weekend. We didn't mind. Jennifer and Arnold had children of their own—two daughters and a son—whose company we enjoyed. With them we watched movies like *Indiana Jones* and *ET*, played in the vines among the forest, and splashed around in the dam on the inner tubes of tyres.

Both daughters were pretty and one of them I had a crush on. She was fair-skinned and freckled, with strawberry blonde hair and light blue eyes. Once I saw her pull down her panties and squat to take a piss in the long grass. She didn't mind me watching.

"Boys have a penis and girls have a fanny," I told her. Of course, I couldn't see her fanny from where I was watching, and I wasn't bold enough to duck down for a closer look. I was damn curious to know what it looked like though.

"That's right," she said, finishing up. She smiled and wiggled her ass as she hitched up her panties. "Girls and boys have different bits."

A moment later her father appeared swinging a bucket of kitchen scraps. He was wearing grease-stained overalls and his long white hair he'd tied back into a ponytail.

He was oblivious to our conversation. He had no idea I wanted to see his daughter's fanny. I was nonetheless intimated by the man. I watched him throw the contents of the bucket on the compost heap, and before he came back, I made sure to be gone.

Before meeting Jennifer and Arnold and staying at their house, I knew nothing about religion. I'd heard my father talk about God on occasion, but not within the context of Christianity specifically. For him God and nature were synonymous. We'd go for walks in the bush and he'd talk about Gaia and Aboriginal nature spirits, pointing out rock formations and trees that resembled human faces. His brand of spirituality was a kind of white guy shamanism, a mishmash of alternative science and New Age philosophy.

In Buddhism, of course, God is neither here nor there. Most Buddhists don't believe in a God, while those that remain open-minded on the matter couldn't give a hoot as to whether he exists or not. His irrelevance within the Buddhist tradition was brought home to me when, as a child, I encountered at Jennifer and Arnold's house my first Bodhisattva statue.

To me it looked alive; animate as opposed to inanimate, this despite the fact that it never once moved or opened its eyes. A figure made entirely of brass, it sat in a meditative posture, with legs crossed and hands clasped together in prayer. It had not one pair of arms but two. The second pair of arms were holding objects I couldn't quite make out. Prayer beads? A lamp?

Around it sat offerings of dried fruit and candy, incense, candles, fresh cut flowers, and tiny bowls of rice and water. Also present were framed photographs of Tibetan Buddhist lamas. On the wall behind the throne hung decorative, colourful cloths featuring elaborate designs and illustrations of deities.

"Is that God?" I asked my mother, pointing to the statue.

"No, it's not God."

She seemed put out by the question, as though I'd suggested something profane. Yet I persisted, determined to get to the bottom of this weird and exotic thing.

"Is he the devil?"

"No, it's not the devil either."

"Is he a good guy or a bad guy?"

She scoffed. "Good and bad are relative terms."

"Oh..."

"He's called Chenrezig, the Buddha of compassion."

"Why does he have four arms?"

"It's symbolic of his ability to help many people at once."

"So he's a superhero, then? Like Batman or Superman?"

My mother gave up at this point, sighing loudly. "Kind of..."

My mother approached Buddhism with a seriousness bordering on dogmatism. As per Jennifer and Arnold's advice, she began meditating once a day, saying her prayers and cultivating mindfulness.

The benefits of mindfulness she raved about, as if it were a spiritual panacea. We'd be sitting around the table eating dinner and she'd tell me and my brother to "eat more mindfully." Or we'd go for a bushwalk and instead of chatting to pass the time she'd advise us to "be mindful and focus on each step."

I began to despise the word "mindful." For me the notion of mindfulness was a complete and utter bore, about as exciting as brushing my teeth each night before bed, which again my mother suggested I do "mindfully." On the other hand, the alleged "powers" that accompanied enlightenment —levitation, telekinesis and clairvoyance—I wanted to know more about. It appealed to my interest in superheroes.

Jennifer, a gregarious woman with huge bosoms, kept a photo on her alter of a Tibetan Buddhist yogi in an alleged state of partial invisibility. I became obsessed with it.

One afternoon, as she and my mother sat in the kitchen drinking hot mugs of chai, I asked her about the photo. I'd plucked it off the altar and had been carrying it around in one hand while eating by means of the other hand a strawberry jam sandwich. There was some jam smeared on the glass of the frame but otherwise I'd taken good care of it.

"I'm so sorry," said my mother to Jennifer. "He should know better than to touch things on the altar. Especially with sticky fingers."

"That's okay," Jennifer replied. Using a wet sponge, she wiped the jam off the glass in one motion. "Good as new."

I turned to Jennifer. "Is the photo real?"

She nodded. "It was taken ten years ago when Arnold and I were travelling through the Himalayas. We stopped in Dharamsala. Stayed there for a couple of weeks in a monastery. Met the Dalai Lama."

"Is the invisible man the Dalai Lama?"

"No, this is a yogi we met. A holy man. Not necessarily an enlightened being, but still highly realised. We saw him perform a number of remarkable feats. He claimed he could turn invisible. Of course, only after I'd taken the photo was I able to verify this."

"So you didn't actually see him turn invisible?"

She cocked her head to the side as she considered my question. "Well...I do recall seeing a bit of haziness around his body. Like the kind of shimmering that appears above a road on a hot day."

"Wow. That's cool."

"It was cool," she agreed. "Being able to turn invisible is not the point of Buddhism though. We Buddhists believe that these powers or abilities arise spontaneously as the practitioner advances towards enlightenment. In the Hindu tradition they're known as siddhis. Ultimately, they're a distraction from awakening, from attaining Buddhahood."

"Enlightenment sounds boring. I'd rather be invisible like Dr Strange."

She laughed, smacking me playfully on the backside. "You should put the photo back, kiddo."

I did as she asked, returning the photo to its position on the shrine. I stood there studying it a while longer. Though Jennifer believed and insisted it were genuine, I had my doubts. I was old enough to realise that photography was only so reliable; that plenty of strange things could appear in photos that weren't necessarily real. In this case, the quality of the photo was so poor, the image as a whole so blurry, that there was no way to know either way.

It still made me wonder, though. I wanted to believe that such men existed. Real-life superheroes. Men who, through years of meditation and other practices, had acquired magical powers, giving them the ability to shape reality as they saw fit.

After all, there was something not right about the world. Beneath the surface of things there lurked a coldness and cruelty, a demon opposed to happiness and human connection. I knew this demon well. It took people over. A shout of anger from my father. A punch in the face from my brother. A taunt from a bully at school. Fear so overwhelming it set my body trembling.

Was there a way to escape from the demon? Could it be outwitted, overcome?

Years later I'd start meditating myself in an attempt to become enlightened. I'd meet Tibetan lamas and monks, and I'd come to believe—at least for a while—that I'd found the truth.

12

—·—

IT WAS THE DAY of the date and I had nothing decent to wear. Even my best clothes—the garments I set aside for special occasions—were beginning to look stale and worn. The several pairs of expensive jeans I owned were faded and thinning at the knees, and most of my button-up shirts had lost their lustre. I needed, at minimum, a decent shirt for the occasion.

As much as I loathed having to think about clothes and fashion, as much as I wanted to convince myself that such superficialities were beneath me, Mark Twain once said that "clothes make the man" and this I knew to be true. It was a rule which, in the realm of romance, was especially pertinent.

Clearly, I needed to resolve my wardrobe situation. Since the date wasn't for several hours, I still had time to buy a new shirt and maybe a couple of other items. This being my plan, I grabbed my wallet and exited the apartment, then began heading up the street in the direction of the local shopping centre.

It was windy, overcast, miserable. Not so much as a speck of sunlight peeking through the clouds. I had come to hate this town, I realised. Not just this town, but Tasmania as a whole. It wasn't just the climate I despised; it was the people as well. To me they all looked the same—fat, dumb, hairy. More animal than human. Dull-eyed philistines whose sole interests in life revolved around food, alcohol, sex and sport.

My problem is that I didn't belong here. I was an outsider. What terrible sin had I committed to end up trapped in such a place? I wondered. Who were these people I lived among? What did it say about me as one fated to live among them?

The automatic door slid open and I entered. Shiny white floors and beige walls. Pop music playing in the background. Lazy weekend shoppers, most of them mums with kids. A few dads looking bored and despondent. Young couples pushing shopping carts loaded with crap— clothes, pillows, flat-packed furniture, microwave ovens. I could only assume they needed all that stuff because they'd recently moved in together. Playing house. Good luck to them.

I approached the men's section and started to browse, making my way up and down the long aisles. Occasionally an item would catch my attention. I'd pause, reach for it, only to realise that the thing looked ugly or ridiculous, or that the fabric felt rough, cheap and nasty.

Out of curiosity I checked the labels— everything was made in either China or Bangladesh. An image appeared in my mind of a sweatshop in Asia: countless rows of women sat at sewing machines, slaving away for minimum wage, the suffering and desperation evident on their faces.

I pushed the image aside, resumed browsing. Better not to think about it, I concluded.

Eventually I found something I liked—a blue dress shirt with faint black stripes. The pants I decided to give a miss—there was nothing in my size; everything was too big and baggy.

I took the shirt to the change room and tried it on, studying my reflection in the full-length mirror. It fitted perfectly, and for a brief moment I felt confident, almost handsome. This feeling was replaced by one of disgust and fear. There were grey streaks in my hair and the grey was spreading. Even worse, my hairline was rapidly receding; I was going bald.

Men age better than women, sure, but an old fuck is an old fuck and that's what I was becoming. We're nothing but biological machines, I thought. Animated meat. Slowly we decay and start to stink and there's not a damn thing we can do about it.

My dreary thoughts were interrupted by a voice in the booth adjacent to mine. It was that of a young woman, probably early-twenties, talking to a friend on the phone. I'd forgotten that the change room was unisex now. Of course, everything was unisex now.

"I'm sick of him," she moaned. "I told him it's over. He hasn't had a job in months... Last night I came home from work and guess what he was doing?... Watching porn! ... Yes, porn... He had his dick out and everything... It was *so* gross... No, he doesn't deserve a second chance... He's *such* a loser... He needs to accept that I've moved on... I can't keep settling for loser guys... I just can't... So guess what we're doing tonight? We're going out... That's right... Girls' night! We're getting wasted... There are going to be lots of cute guys there..."

The act of eavesdropping on a woman in her twenties made me feel like a dirty old man, though the sense of shame wasn't so great as to prevent me from continuing. There was no further mention of the breakup or the porn-addicted boyfriend. The dull bitch had changed the topic. Disappointed, I tucked the shirt under my arm and left.

I was halfway towards the checkout when I started to have second thoughts about the shirt. I wasn't sure why I'd chosen it. It was a cheap piece of shit. Mass produced garbage. It would rapidly decay like all of my other cheap shirts. The decision was easy to make: I would return it, wear one of my old shirts to the date instead.

I paused, turned around, and headed back to the men's section, placing the shirt on the rack where I'd found it.

As I was about to exit the store, I was stopped by a middle-aged female clerk with a bulldoggish face. "Do you have a receipt?" she asked. "I can't let you leave unless you show a receipt."

"No," I replied. "I didn't buy anything."

She scrutinised me suspiciously with dull, beady eyes. This went on for some time.

"I was about to buy an item but I put it back," I added.

Keeping her eyes fixed on me, she shifted her weight from one foot to the other, causing her large bosoms to wobble beneath her uniform. "I'm letting you off this once. Next time I want to see a receipt."

"Even if I don't make a purchase?"

She said nothing, merely stood there with a blank expression, a robot unable to compute the situation as a consequence of inadequate hardware. A few seconds passed before she gave a response: "Next time I want to see a receipt."

I shook my head and walked out the door.

13

I ENDED UP DRESSING in jeans, a red flannelette shirt, and a black leather jacket. I also wore my best pair of shoes, which I polished to a fine shine. Aiming to look just a little bit younger, I chose to ditch the flatcap and instead style my hair with wax.

I looked okay. Good enough for the purpose of a first date.

On the way over I stopped off at the bakery and bought a loaf of French bread. I figured I needed to contribute something; and since I assumed that like many Christians Peter and June eschewed alcohol, bread was the next logical choice.

Their house was situated at the end of a cul-de-sac, in a suburb noted for its affluent dwellings. It looked almost new. The walls were of rendered brick, painted white, and the roof tiled. Bay windows looked out onto a sprawling front yard, which featured a flawless lawn and white-pebbled gardens. The driveway was wide enough to accommodate multiple cars, so I parked there.

I climbed three steps to a wooden deck, rang the bell, waited. I wondered if my date was here already. There was one other car in the driveway besides mine and this I identified as belonging to Peter and June, so most likely not.

It was Peter who answered the door. He wore black tracksuit pants and a green polo shirt and his forehead glistened with perspiration. He said hello, smiled and motioned me inside. "Apologies for my appearance. I was just on the exercise bike."

I stepped inside and he closed the door behind us.

"No apology necessary. You know, I've recently started working out myself and I have to say it's changed my life."

He dabbed at his forehead with a hand towel. "That's great, Chuck. Going to church *and* working out. Sounds as though the Lord's really blessing you at this moment."

"I'm not sure the Lord's got a lot to do with it," I joked. "I'm the one doing the hard work."

He smiled and winked. "Don't be so certain. To quote the Apostle Paul, 'For it is God who works in you, both to will and to work for his good pleasure.'"

He led me into the kitchen where, after handing him the bread, I positioned a stool and sat down. It was spacious, modern, one of the finest kitchens I'd ever seen. The benchtops were of grey marble, the cabinets stainless steel, and the cookware that hung from above was of shiny copper. The walls were tiled in a combination of ceramic aqua-green and pearly white. A large gas oven with six burners sat at the rear, a sturdy beast of a thing. These people had it made.

There was a chicken roasting in the oven. It smelt good. June was chopping ingredients for a salad. When she was saw me she put down the knife and said, "Good to see you, Chuck."

"You too. Thanks for inviting me."

"Anything I can get you to drink?" asked Peter.

"Water's fine."

"Sure."

From a jug he poured a tall glass of chilled water, placing it on the benchtop in front of me. I get thirsty when I'm nervous. I raised it to my lips and drank the entire contents in several gulps.

He sat down on the stool beside me. "Stephanie texted to say that she's held up at work. I'm sure she'll be here soon though."

I realised I didn't particularly like the name "Stephanie." It was slightly better than "Megan," but not by much. Both names I'd come to associate with humourless career women. I hoped this Stephanie was different.

For the next ten minutes Peter showed me around the house. It was only a rental, he explained, but pretty soon he and June planned to buy a place of their own. They desperately wanted children, maybe a dog. The former they'd been trying for, but so far without success.

We ended up seated on the couch in his study. One of the prettiest rooms in the house, it overlooked the rear courtyard—a paved area featuring a birdbath and several garden statues, and to my relief, not a single gnome.

I glanced across at the bookshelf in the corner, scrutinising the titles stacked neatly on its shelves. There were a number of medical textbooks, along with numerous works by N. T. Wright and C. S. Lewis, not to mention several translations of the Bible. That Peter evidently appreciated books made me respect him even more.

Though there were several paintings mounted on the walls, all of them Christian-themed, one in particular caught my attention. It depicted Jesus seated on a rock surrounded by smiling and adoring children.

That Jesus had a soft spot for children—though thankfully not in a weird way—is evident in the Bible. I did wonder though: if the guy came back and children started flocking to him, how long would it take before someone accused him of being a paedophile?

"June is jealous that I chose this as my study," laughed Peter. "She says it's the best room in the house."

"She's not wrong." There was a pause, then I asked, "You spend a lot of time here?"

He nodded. "It's where I come to reflect and relax."

"You don't strike me as the kind of person who has difficulty relaxing. You're so calm. So cheerful. How do you do it?"

He laughed. I could tell he was flattered by the comment, yet slightly embarrassed as well. "It's not as though I have it all figured out, Chuck."

I nodded to the painting of Jesus. "You have Jesus in your life. That's positive. He had it all figured out, right?" The comment came out more sarcastic than intended and I instantly regretted saying it.

Peter's expression and tone became serious. "Jesus is the way, the truth and the life. He came here to save humanity from sin, to set us on the right path. It's easy to think that we can do it alone. But we can't do it alone. The world is troubled and people are corrupt, and our only salvation is through Jesus. There is no other way."

"Maybe there is no salvation. Maybe all we have is this troubled world. And maybe once we die, that's it."

"That's a bleak way of looking at things. The events in the Bible paint a very different picture. In the gospels we have multiple, independent testimonies that all point to the same truth: that Jesus was a real person, born to a virgin; that he walked on water and performed other miracles, and that after he was crucified he came back to life."

"It's a nice story, Peter, and I wish I could believe it. The problem for me is that I wasn't there and never met the man. I never saw Jesus walk on water or feed 5,000 people with five loaves and two fish. Why, then, should I accept the claim that he is the literal son of God, as opposed to someone who was very clever, wise and charismatic?"

"Christianity doesn't demand that we have blind faith. We're encouraged to test the word of God, to exercise our discernment."

"So tell me, have you ever doubted your faith?"

"Of course. Many times. I'm a former atheist. I used to laugh at Christians."

"What changed your mind?"

"It was a combination of factors, not just one. I started reading the Bible, started going to church. What clinched it for me was when I came face to face with the suffering of the world. You see, I used to think we humans had it all figured out, that through science, technology, medicine, we'd eventually manage to solve all of our problems and create a perfect society. When I looked deeper, I realised I was mistaken. I recognised that this is a fallen world, a world of wickedness and corruption, exactly as the Bible says. And it's not because of external factors. It's because of us, because of original sin. But what's broken can be fixed. There's hope. Jesus is that hope."

Just then I heard the doorbell chime and the front door open.

"Must be Stephanie," said Peter.

I followed him out into the kitchen, where Stephanie and June were already busy chatting.

She was pretty and petite, with green eyes, a V-shaped chin, and shoulder-length, wavy red hair. Her legs I could barely see, although their smooth, slender shape was easy to discern beneath the thin fabric of her light blue dress. Her small feet I was able to appreciate because she wore leather sandals and the straps were thin.

She had in her hand a stick of lip gloss. This she applied to her sensual lips then placed in the handbag in front of her, snapping it closed. As I approached to introduce myself, she regarded me with a look of hesitant interest.

"Nice to meet you. I'm Chuck."

She smiled. "Likewise. I'm Stephanie."

I liked her vibe already. Her sophistication was balanced by a feminine playfulness that I found both intoxicating and mysterious. Here was a woman, I thought, who knew how to enjoy herself but whose idea of fun didn't fit the common mould.

In the dining room we sat down to eat—me and Stephanie on one side of the table, June and Peter on the other. I was about to sink my teeth into a chicken drumstick when I noticed that the others had their eyes closed and their hands together in prayer. Blushing with shame, I put down the drumstick and followed suit.

It was Peter who did the honours. "O Lord, we thank you for the gifts of your bounty which we enjoy at this table. As you have provided for us in the past, so may you sustain us throughout our lives. While we enjoy your gifts, may we never forget the needy and those in want."

We said "Amen" in unison. It sounded strange when I said it: too faint, almost feminine. I felt embarrassed.

Stephanie turned to me and said, "Tell me about yourself, Chuck."

"I write. I have a young son. I keep busy. Recently I've started exploring Christianity. What about yourself?"

"I'm a parent as well. I have a daughter. Kate. She's seven. How old is your son?"

"He's four. Turning five soon."

"Oh, lovely. They're adorable at that age."

She brought out her phone and showed me some photos of Kate—a little, blonde-haired girl with a beaming smile. I showed her some photos of my son. She said he was cute.

I wanted to avoid the topic of my job. Saying you're a freelance journalist and author has no currency in our society. It's equivalent to saying you're lazy and live on welfare. Hardly the way to impress a potential girlfriend.

To my relief, the conversation drifted to the topic of Stephanie's job, not mine. Previously a bookkeeper, she now worked as an accountant; a profession she'd pursued following her divorce. She pointed out the difficulties of juggling both motherhood and a full-time career. To cope, she relied heavily on babysitters and childcare services.

The father of her child, a successful lawyer, she had almost no contact with. He'd since moved to Sydney and remarried, seeing his daughter only once or twice a year. Though Stephanie didn't go so far as to explicitly speak ill of her ex, I inferred from the way she described him that she still harboured feelings of resentment towards the man. I gathered it was he who'd initiated the divorce, trading her in for a younger woman.

Realising I'd been overly focused on Stephanie and that I ought to open up the conversation to include Peter and June, I asked the three of them how they'd met.

It was Peter who spoke first. "Funnily enough it happened on the side of the road."

Stephanie laughed, then began to described the incident. "I was driving with a trailer attached to my car. This was shortly after my divorce. Rather than hire a removalist, I figured I'd do the moving myself. Stupid idea of course! So there I am on the main street of town, trying to park the thing, not knowing what on earth I'm doing—since I've never driven with a trailer before—and my car's pointed in one direction and the trailer the other. I'm holding up traffic and it's absolute chaos."

"We come to the rescue," laughed June.

"You did," agreed Stephanie. She turned to me. "June and Peter were the only ones who helped. Everyone else was honking and shouting. June got out, started directing traffic. Peter—thank God—got behind the wheel of my car and managed to park the thing. So, yeah, they saved my ass that day."

Said Peter, "A week later we met up for lunch, I think?"

"We did," said Stephanie. "I invited the two of you out for lunch because I wanted to thank you both for your marvellous help."

"Yet it wasn't quite the conversation you expected," said Peter, smiling at the memory.

"No, it wasn't. Thanks to you and June, we spoke about Jesus and little else. Not that I minded, of course."

"So you're a Christian now?" I asked.

"Not quite. I'm an aspiring Christian."

"We haven't quite managed to convince her," laughed Peter.

"I do believe in God, though," added Stephanie. "And I've started reading the Bible daily."

"I'm in a similar position," I said, "although I wouldn't say I believe in God; I'm not quite ready to take that leap. I'm in the process of putting Christianity to the test. I've explored just about every other religion, so I figured why not Christianity."

"Weren't you a Buddhist previously?" asked Peter.

"No. My mother is a Buddhist, and growing up I spent a lot of time around Buddhism. But I never became a Buddhist myself."

June stood up and began to clear the table. A moment later Peter rose to help. After they'd left and were busying themselves in the kitchen, Stephanie leaned towards me and said, "Buddhism, eh? How intriguing. So why didn't you become a Buddhist?"

"Well, I think there's a lot of value in Buddhism. I never really took to it, though. Philosophically it always struck me as vague, wishy-washy. Buddhism basically says, 'Be a compassionate person. Meditate every day. Don't kill animals and insects. Oh, and if you manage to attain enlightenment in the process, well done. If not, there's always next lifetime. Or the one after that.'"

She laughed. "I see your point. So why Christianity now?"

I shrugged. "As I said, I'm approaching it as an experiment. I should ask you the same question: why Christianity?"

She brushed her hair away from her eyes and was silent for a moment, thinking. "Peter and June's influence has had a lot to do with it. They're amazing people. One of the nicest couples I've ever met. If that's the influence of Christianity, if it really does make people kinder and happier, then there must be some truth at the core of it. Don't you think?"

I nodded. She was right about Peter and June. So far, my interactions with Christians had been overwhelmingly positive, and in general I'd come to consider them of good character and high moral standing. Yet I'd also met some weird Christians. Here I thought of Frank and Barbara and their pornographic gnomes. The image made me shudder.

I heard Stephanie's phone beep; it was a text message. After reading it, she sighed and said, "It's the babysitter. Apparently Kate's refusing to go to bed. I'd better get home. Though it's been nice meeting you, Chuck. Let's catch up for coffee sometime and continue this conversation."

I wasted little time in getting her number, not quite believing my good fortune that the date had been a success and that Stephanie sincerely wanted to see me again. Maybe, I thought, if I played my cards right, I'd finally have a woman in my life once more.

14

THERE WAS A WORD document open on the screen in front of me and all I could do was stare blankly at it as the minutes ticked by. I'd been commissioned to write an article on the late Canadian journalist Joe Fisher. So far, though, I'd only written a couple of paragraphs. The required word count was 4,500 and I had a mere four days to write the damn thing.

The words weren't coming. Mentally I felt blocked. The creative process isn't something you can force. Well actually you can, but the work suffers. Same goes with romance.

Once more I thought about Stephanie. She'd been on my mind since the date three days ago, and as of yet I hadn't contacted her to line up a second date. The reason for this was simple: I was worried I might come across as desperate, worried she might say "no."

Did she actually like me, I wondered? Or was she simply being polite when she suggested we get together again?

The conversation, I thought, had gone well. I hadn't said anything stupid and for the most part I'd been articulate and engaging. As for Stephanie, she was clearly an intelligent woman and not one to shy away from big and important topics like religion. This I admired about her.

Yet, as I'd discovered from experience, it's one thing to stimulate a woman's intellect and a different thing entirely to stimulate not only her intellect but her emotions and her desires as well.

The problem is, I was good at being friends with women but not so good at seducing them and making them want to have sex with me. Though not a complete failure in the realm of romance, I was no Don Juan either. Not even close.

Following my divorce, I'd dated a little. None of these relationships had worked out though. Dating gets harder with age. Compared to when you're younger, the attraction is less, the passion barely present, and at that age your lives are so stressful and complicated that you hardly have time for one another. Especially when there are children involved.

I couldn't help but wonder: If I dated Stephanie, would it end the same way?

Fuck it, I thought, time for a break.

I stood up, stretched, visited the toilet. In the kitchen I made myself a cup of tea. I craved sugar, but didn't add any. I'd stopped adding sugar to my tea and coffee when I'd noticed it was making me fat, giving me a belly. As you age your metabolism slows down and you put on weight easier. Was this my life now? No sugar? No fun?

I returned to the office a few minutes later, closing the door to minimise distraction. The hot cup of tea I placed on the desk in front of me. Again I tried to write, but again the words refused to come.

Sighing loudly in defeat, I saved and closed the word document. Despite the looming deadline, I wasn't worried. The article I'd manage to finish on time, even if it meant a few late nights.

I turned away from the screen of my computer and gazed out the window at the distant ocean. Along the horizon dark clouds were building into a thunderstorm. Typically such storms would sweep across the horizon before vanishing into the distance, not quite reaching the town itself. If they did happen to approach, they were short-lived; storms weaken over land.

Pity, I thought, I enjoy a good thunderstorm. If I had my way, not only would the storm draw near, it'd engulf us. It would tear this town apart and set it on fire—shops, houses, everything. Thunder like the sound of exploding bombs. Apocalyptic lightning shot from the blazing eyes of God. Something to make the Christians cream their jeans over.

Finally I knew what I had to do. I swung around in my chair and picked up my phone. The text message I kept deliberately short: "Hi Stephanie. Free to catch up for coffee this weekend?"

I hit send, mentally crossing my fingers as I did so. I waited with bated breath for her response. It came less than two minutes later: "Absolutely I'm free. How about Saturday at 11am?"

15

STILL CHEWING A BITE of toasted sandwich, Brian asked, "How old is she?"

He'd invited me out for lunch and insisted on paying. I'd wanted to decline the invitation. Yet, in a way, I'd come to enjoy Brian's company and to disappoint him or hurt his feelings was, I felt, out of the question.

"About the same age as me. Late-thirties."

With food still in his mouth, he raised the mug of coffee to his lips and drank, slurping loudly. The man had no table manners. He may have been a child of God, but he was first and foremost an animal.

"Is she Christian?"

"Kind of."

"What do you mean 'kind of?'"

"Well, she believes in God, and she goes to church occasionally, but she doesn't make a big song and dance about it."

I was about to add "unlike you Pentecostal Christians," but I didn't need to; Brian already knew to which group I was referring.

He laughed. "We do know how to worship with passion, I'll say that. It's the only way to worship, as far as I'm concerned. God created us! He created this beautiful blue planet! How awesome is that, Chuck? Isn't that something to be celebrated?!"

I gazed into the last dregs of my hot chocolate—a tepid, creamy mess at the bottom of my mug. I looked over at Brian. "I'm not sure it's something to be celebrated. It's a remarkable world, I agree, but it's also deeply flawed and filled with suffering. So, in that sense, God has a lot to answer for."

Brian's eyes widened. "You'll anger God if you talk like that. I hope you're not being serious."

"Look, I'm saying there's a lot to admire about the world. The sun shines and the birds twitter. But I'd be denying half of reality if I didn't also acknowledge the darkness."

"You're talking about good and evil? Darkness and light?"

"I suppose."

Brian put down his mug of coffee, then reached for his phone. It contained a digital copy of the Bible, from which he read aloud the following quote: "I am the light of the world. Whoever follows me will not walk in darkness, but will have the light of life."

"From John, right?"

"John chapter eight, verse twelve."

I shrugged. "And?"

Brian opened his arms. "Don't you get it? It's revolutionary! Jesus came to earth to fulfil an important mission. The most important mission ever. He was sent by God to guide humanity out of the darkness."

"And yet we're still caught in darkness, aren't we?"

Brian leaned forward and conspiratorially whispered, "It's Satan who's responsible for the darkness."

"Really? Or is what we call 'Satan' an aspect of human nature? Solzhenitsyn famously said that the line separating good and evil passes through the heart of every human being, and I think he was right."

"Ah, that's because of original sin. Humanity was perfect to begin with. We were one with God in the garden and we lacked for nothing. Until one day Satan appeared as a serpent and tempted Eve to eat from the Tree of Knowledge of Good and Evil. Adam also took a bite from the apple. They disobeyed God. When God found out..."

"—He punished Adam and Eve by expelling them from the garden. Since the fall, we no longer have the gift of eternal life, and we're forced to toil away on earth and suffer and die... Yes, I've read Genesis, Brian."

"If you've read the New Testament as well..."

"—I have."

"Okay, then you'd know that Genesis is part of a much longer story, a story that's still ongoing. In the New Testament we're told that Jesus was sent by God to save humanity, to free us from sin. We're also told he'll appear again, although we don't know the day or the hour of his coming. The completion of the story will be the restoration of God's kingdom. Heaven and earth united! Imagine that?"

"I'd like to imagine it, but I can't," I said. "To me it sounds too good to be true."

"What's holding you back, Chuck? All you need to do is allow Jesus into your heart. It's as simple as that."

I laughed. "I wish it were as simple as that. All this talk of other realities, other worlds. Sounds wonderful. The only world I know is this one though. The fallen world."

Brian finished the last of his coffee in one mighty gulp, then reached for a serviette. After using it to wipe the edges of his mouth, he scrunched it into a tight ball. This he placed delicately on the edge of his saucer, as if it were an origami crane. "You're about to go on a date with a high-quality woman. Good things are happening in your life. You should be happy, grateful."

"I am grateful. It's only a date though. It may not lead to an actual relationship."

"Personally I think it's the work of God, the two of you coming together."

"Of course you'd think that," I joked. "You assume that every good thing is the work of God."

Together we rose and headed to the counter. Behind the cash register stood a young woman— no older than twenty-five—with bright purple hair, a ring through one nostril, and the symbol of a hammer and sickle tattooed on her left shoulder. She was neither friendly nor rude but emotionally absent, simply doing her job. Stretched tight across her pointed breasts was a *Black Lives Matter* t-shirt.

Was she a radical leftist, I wondered? Or was her style simply that of a young person trying to stand out and gain attention by pretending to support trendy political causes?

Brian paid the bill and we left. Once we were out the door and making our way down the street, I turned to him and facetiously asked, "Why didn't you talk to her about Jesus?"

He shook his head. "Oh, no. Lost cause that one. Not once have I had any luck with dyed-haired women. Not once."

"Really? And why do you think that is?"

"You know those poisonous frogs in the Amazon, the ones with bright-coloured skin?"

I nodded.

"Well, it's the same with women. If she has bright hair, she's likely to be toxic, poisonous and dangerous; and as a Christian man you'd be wise to give her a wide berth."

"Are you implying that dyed-haired women are beyond redemption?"

We stopped at an intersection. I hit the button to cross the road. The vast majority of shoppers were elderly men and women dressed in thick coats and scarves, their attention scattered and life-force waning. The forgotten, invisible members of society.

Finally Brian looked at me and replied, "It's not my fault if they're going to hell."

The walking man turned green and we crossed.

"Hell, really? For having dyed hair?"

"It's the destructive influence of feminism. Feminism has made women ugly, rude, more like men. Turned the sexes against each other. It's an inversion of what's natural and good. It's Satanism, pure and simple."

"So you believe in traditional gender roles, then? Men as providers, woman as housewives and mothers?"

"Absolutely, it's the only way."

"Fair enough. But society has changed a lot over the decades. This isn't the 1950s anymore. We're living in a different era."

He shrugged. "That's the problem. The natural order of the world had been lost. God will set things right, though. It's just a matter of time."

We said our goodbyes and parted ways, walking off in opposite directions. After a while I stopped, glanced back. From this distance he looked small, sad, helpless. Another lonely old man, I thought, trapped in an era long gone and unable to adapt to the modern world. Then it occurred to me: if I wasn't careful, if I didn't play my cards right, it's exactly what I would become.

16

FOR SOME REASON I kept having strange and very vivid dreams. I felt that the dreams were trying to tell me something, but I never managed to figure out what; deciphering their symbolism proved impossible. They'd leave me wracking my brain for an answer or an explanation, often for days even weeks on end.

In one such dream I was a teenager back at high school, and while strolling down the hallway after class I came face to face with none other than the late Charles Bukowski. There was no one else around; they'd all left. It was just me and the famous author, two lonely souls in the dreamworld, not quite sure what to make of each other.

He glanced up as I approached, nodded hello. I nodded hello back. He was dressed as a janitor, in green overalls and a cap. There was a cigarette dangling from the corner of his scowling mouth, and he was holding a mop. His skin was all pockmarked and dimpled and he looked ugly as hell. I could barely believe how ugly he looked.

For a while I stood there watching him mop the floor, humbled to be in his presence, yet unsure whether to remain, lest I distract him from his work. Every now and then he'd sigh in complaint or pause to run a hand through his sweat drenched hair. The poor old guy was exhausted. They were running him ragged.

Finally he stopped, bringing the mop to an upright position. His belly and chest heaved in and out as he struggled to catch his breath, and, leaning against the mop, he turned to me and asked, "Why are you still here?" He hissed his words like a snake, leaving no pause between them. It's not so much that he sounded unfriendly, but tired, irritated, over it.

"I think I'm lost," I answered.

"It's after hours and you're not supposed to be here."

"Sorry."

"Never mind. I was about to go on my break anyway. Join me."

He leaned the mop against one of the lockers, then wiped his palms on the sides of his filthy overalls. "Come on," he said, motioning for me to follow.

Together we strode down the dimly-lit hallway. It stretched on and on, like an endless cavern deep below the earth. Was this my high school, I wondered? Or had I ended up in hell? Or were the two places one and the same?

Once we reached the boys' toilet, he stopped and turned to face me. "I gotta drain the lizard. We haven't got much time, so let's piss and talk."

I felt uncomfortable following him into the toilet, but follow I did. It was a typical high school bathroom: stalls, urinals, sinks, white tiles. The place filthy and lacking soap. Many of the tiles were cracked and covered in graffiti of giant dicks and hairy vaginas drawn in black, permanent marker.

Hanging back near the door, I watched Bukowski approached one of the urinals. Without so much as a hint of embarrassment, he unzipped his fly in front of me and let loose, emitting an involuntary fart as his piss hit the porcelain bowl.

"Gee that feels good," he sighed. "I've mentioned how much I enjoy a good beer shit. A beer piss isn't in the same league, but it's definitely up there with life's great pleasures."

"Was there something you wanted to tell me?" I asked.

"Yes. I need to talk to you about God and women."

"Which one?"

"Let's start with God and not bother with women."

"Okay."

Finished, he shook his cock, zipped up his fly, and flushed the urinal. I held open the door as we exited together. I wasn't at all surprised that he hadn't washed his hands; this was Bukowski, after all. Hardly a shining example of good hygiene and fine manners.

Once again I followed him down the hallway. This time we took a left into the gym. It was all lit up—the basketball hoops, the polished wooden floor, the rows of plastic seats. We sat side by side at the very back where the incandescent lighting wasn't so glaringly bright.

"Let's get real about God," said Bukowski. He had in his hand a bottle of beer. He twisted the top, threw away the cap, took a long swig.

"The first thing you need to know about God," he continued, "is that he benefits from the blindness and ignorance of that which he has created. The same way a stage magician earns his livelihood from pulling the wool over the eyes of his audience. If they knew how he performed his tricks, it wouldn't be much of a magic show, now would it? And would he get paid?"

"I guess not."

"Of course he wouldn't: he'd be out of a job! Now, as an art form, magic is challenging, risky. Magicians are continually refining their acts, and even the most accomplished magician will occasionally slip up. The same goes for God. When necessary, he course corrects, not always delicately. Think about it: God creates man and the animals. But it ends up being a disaster, a mess. So what does he do? He hits the reset button. He floods the earth, wipes the slate clean. Mass slaughter. Except Noah and his family, of course, along with two of each animal. He spared Noah. God has his favourites, see?"

"It does seem harsh and unfair."

Bukowski took a long swig, then burped; then drained the last dregs of his beer and burped again. "Forget about harsh and unfair. That's beside the point. My point is that God has his own agenda, and it has nothing to do with human happiness. Each life he creates he regards as an experiment. You're an experiment. I'm an experiment. My damn cat is an experiment."

"Is that such a bad thing, being an experiment?"

Suddenly his face turned red with anger and he pitched the empty beer bottle into the air. It sailed over the rows of seats in front of us, landing in the middle of the basketball court with a smash.

He looked at me with eyes wild. "That was an experiment. See what happened? Not such a good outcome for the bottle, now was it?"

"The bottle's broken," I said, stating the obvious.

"The bottle's fucked."

"I think I get your point. Not all experiments end well."

"Some do. Some don't. All depends."

"What about your life? Was it a successful experiment or not? You became famous. Surely that's not such a bad outcome?"

Bukowski rested his elbows on his knees and looked me square in the eyes, his expression one of utter seriousness. I felt scared, intimidated; I was worried he might beat me up or throw another bottle. Finally his face softened and he said, "I became famous because of my writing; but for my writing I paid a price, and that price was suffering."

"Sounds awful," I replied.

He shrugged. "It would've been worse had my suffering amounted to nothing."

"So now what?" I asked. "Why do you spend your days mopping floors?"

"Easy. Service to God."

"Here in purgatory?"

"Purgatory or hell. Same thing." He leaned back in his chair, put his arms behind his head. "It's not as bad as it sounds. I get to drink and write, although I have to say I'm running out of things to write about. I like the peace, the quiet, the solitude. I work five days a week, get the weekends off. I'm allowed visitors, including whores."

"At least there's beer and whores," I remarked.

He belched loudly, then nodded.

At that moment the dream ended.

17

ON THE DAY OF the date with Stephanie I decided to arrive a little early. We'd agreed to meet at the café at 11:00, so instead I showed up at 10:30. I figured the extra half-hour would give me time to scout the venue, choose a nice table, order a coffee, and be seated comfortably when she walked in.

Ironically, and quite without thinking about it, the venue we chose was called the Buddha Café. Located adjacent to a nursery, it occupied a shady spot surrounded by trees and ferns, the grounds of the garden decorated by water features, Buddha statues, wind chimes, and colourful Tibetan prayer flags.

Inside were dozens of crystal lamps, singing bowls and other New Age knickknacks. I found the décor over the top and off-putting. The purpose of a café is to serve coffee, not positive vibes, crystal healing, and fairy dust. But such is the state of our society, where spirituality has been turned into a commodity and nothing of true value remains.

It turned out my plan to arrive early had backfired; Stephanie was already here. She sat at a table at the very back, opposite a short woman with straight black hair. They were talking loudly, in a highly animated fashion. The friend was the loudest. She kept laughing and saying "I know, I know. Can you believe it?"

I hung back, not sure what to do. I hadn't been expecting this. Who in their right mind would show up to a date not alone but accompanied by a friend? It didn't make sense. Unless they wished to send the message that it wasn't a date after all. Could that be Stephanie's intention, I wondered?

I considered doing a runner, simply walking out before Stephanie spotted me and texting to say I couldn't make it. I stood there glued to the spot in a state of indecisiveness. At that moment the friend looked at me and I heard her say to Stephanie, "Is that him?"

Too late. I'd been spotted.

"Chuck?" said Stephanie, turning to look at me.

Was she put out by my being here this early, I wondered? Maybe a little, though I couldn't tell for sure.

I walked over to their table, said hello. I stood there with my hands in the pockets of my jacket, shifting my weight slightly from one foot to the other, trying my best—but failing—to mask my anxiety.

"We thought we'd have lunch before you arrived," said Stephanie. "I wasn't expecting you here this early."

I was pissed off but I didn't let it show. "I can come back later if you'd like? Let you two finish up?"

She waved the suggestion away with her hand. "Oh, no. It's fine. Jane and I were just making girl talk. Please join us."

I pulled out a chair, sat down. "Secret women's business, eh?"

"We were talking about her ex-husband."

Jane laughed. "The bastard, you mean."

The two resumed talking about "the bastard" while I periodically scrolled through my phone and pretended not to listen. Jane, it emerged, was a mother of two boys—aged seven and nine—of whom she shared custody with her ex-husband. She described him in such unflattering terms as to conjure in my mind the image of a creature with the same level of sophistication as one of those idiot TV dads from an early-90s American sitcom.

I politely excused myself, heading to the desk to order a coffee. Normally I pay on a first date, but Stephanie already had a coffee, so I didn't bother to ask if she wanted another. When, some ten minutes later, I returned to the table with my beverage, the topic of conversation was still focused on "the bastard."

"He knows that Michael gets a bad case of the farts when he drinks full cream milk," moaned Jane. "But he gives it to him anyway."

"Have you suggested alternatives?" asked Stephanie. "Soy? Almond? Lactose free?"

"Yes. I even went to the trouble of buying two cartons of soy and placing them in Michael's bag. I gave Daniel specific instructions to make sure Michael drank the soy. He agreed. Then guess what?"

"What?"

"I picked up Michael and Sam on the Sunday. I looked through Michael's bag and the soy was still there. Both cartons. Completely untouched."

"No!"

"Yes! The next thing I know, I'm driving down the highway and Michael starts farting in the backseat. Really cranking them out. Smelt like something had died."

"That's terrible, Jane. And very irresponsible of Daniel."

"I'll say. He clearly doesn't care about his son's health. Takes no responsibility. And I'm the one who has to deal with the farts."

Stephanie turned to me and asked, "You're a single father, Chuck. What are your thoughts?"

Oh boy. I had plenty of thoughts on the topic, but I didn't want to share them. I thought, in particular, that Jane was a whinging cunt and that her ex-husband deserved a medal for putting up with the bitch.

I put down my coffee, cleared my throat and in a weak voice said, "In the case of shared custody, there are lots of compromises to be made. It can be very challenging."

I was trying to play it safe, and the remark was the best I could manage under the circumstances.

Jane emitted a trill laugh. "I hope you're not taking my ex-husband's side."

"Not at all," I replied, knowing I'd put my foot in it and not sure how to wipe the turd from my shoe. "What I meant to say is that it's not always obvious what one parent expects from the other parent. Clear communication can be a real issue."

Jane offered no comment, tightening her lips together in obvious disagreement. Clutching her handbag, she rose from her chair and in a voice thick with condescension said, "I need to go, though I wish you two the very best with your date." She left hastily, making a beeline for the door.

"I apologise for my friend," said Stephanie. "She can be a little intense, but she means well."

"She's certainly intense," I agreed.

"I apologise, too, if the date's already off to an awkward start."

"It isn't," I lied.

Stephanie rested her arms on the table and leaned forward. It was a "let's get down to brass tacks" kind of look. A hint of cleavage was visible through a fold in her button-up shirt and for the first time I noticed that she had nice breasts; large but not overly so. The bra was frilly, dark red, the naughty kind of lingerie as opposed to the functional kind.

Noticing myself staring, I blinked and shifted my gaze. I hoped Stephanie hadn't noticed.

"So we've covered religion," she said. "What about work? You haven't told me much about your job."

"There's not a lot to say. I'm a freelance journalist and author. I write books, articles, the occasional piece of fiction."

"Does it pay okay? I imagine it's hard to make a living as a writer."

"It depends. Popular magazines can pay quiet well. Obscure magazines pay almost nothing. The best paid work is ghost writing."

"I'm impressed. I doubt I'd be able to handle the stress of working for myself, without a regular income to rely on. Do you ever long for a regular job?"

"No. I've worked regular jobs in the past. Office jobs. Factory jobs. They bore me. The money's better than writing—almost everything pays better than writing—but the nine-to-five grind isn't for me. I love what I do. Wouldn't give it up for anything."

"Good for you. I admire people with creative talent. Can't say I'm very creative myself. Kate is, though, she loves drawing."

"So is my son."

"Tell me, does he still draw those pictures of the three of you together: mother, father, child?"

I nodded. "That's about all he draws. He recently drew me a Father's Day card with three stick figures on it. We look like potatoes and we all have smiling faces. Almost broke my heart. I don't think he's quite accepted that we're no longer a family. What about Kate?"

She was silent for a moment, gazing off into space, her hands wrapped tightly around the empty mug in front of her. This time when she spoke her voice sounded strained. "She still struggles with it, same as your son."

There was melancholy in the woman, deep and wide like a lake. To what extent had her heart been broken, I wondered? It was obvious she loved and cared deeply about her daughter. But what about the capacity to love another man? Had that died along with her marriage?

All of a sudden she emitted a droll laugh and her eyes met mine directly. "Gosh, we're a cheery bunch, aren't we, Chuck! Talking about divorce on what's supposed to be a date."

Struck by the awkwardness of the situation, I laughed too. "I admit my dating skills are a little on the rusty side."

"No, it's not your fault. I was the one who brought up the topic of divorce, not you. And I must again apologise for my friend earlier."

"Please, don't apologise."

There was nothing happy to talk about, nothing more to say to one other. The date had gone poorly and there was little possibility—or point—of another. It therefore surprised me when, shortly before we parted ways, Stephanie said, "Let's do dinner sometime. My place."

I nodded. "Sure. I'd like that."

18

SHORTLY AFTER MY PARENTS divorced and my mother moved out, my father remarried. It happened in a matter of months: gone with the old mum, in with the new. Not that she wanted the role of stepmother, or indeed truly adopted it.

Her name was Sally. A dark-haired woman with pale skin, freckles and sharp, hazel eyes, she emanated a lack of warmth and engagement with the world. Eventually I'd come to think of her as a witch.

Prior to moving in with us, she'd lived in Sydney, where she'd tried to eke out a living as an artist specialising in Japanese wood-prints. Her personality was in keeping with the profession to which she aspired—quiet, serious, introverted, reserved. When she laughed—which was almost never—it emanated not from the belly but from high in the throat. It was a pretend laugh.

Sally, I could tell, pretended a lot. She pretended to like me and my brother. She pretended to love our father. She pretended to enjoy living with us.

It was all an act, a façade. I saw through her skilful performance but my father didn't.

Neither my father nor Sally had a job, and for the first six months of their relationship they rarely left their bedroom. Late at night and early in the morning, and occasionally during the middle of the day, moans and other weird noises drifted muffled through the thin walls and under the crack of their door.

Sounds of pleasure or sounds of pain? Both my brother and I wondered about this. We quickly learned to keep our distance and not place any demands on our father, remaining seen but not heard.

Sally loathed children and found them annoying, and it wasn't long before she began to scold us for what she perceived as a lack of cleanliness and good manners on our part. Small incidents angered her—for example, a dirty knife left near the sink, or a sprinkling of bread crumbs on the kitchen bench.

That we disliked her healthy cooking—her tofu salads, pumpkin pastas and spinach bakes—further cemented her opinion of us as "problem children." Behind our father's back she teased us and called us names, "dirty little pigs" being one of her favourites. These incidents we kept to ourselves.

She became in our eyes a creature to be feared and avoided, more monster than human. We learned to tread carefully around her, to hide our feelings, to play it safe. We tried our best to eliminate mistakes that could potentially make us a target of her unpredictable moods and sudden bursts of anger. The kitchen we began to keep spotless. Our bedrooms too.

Sally was an expert at dissimulation. Yet even the very best façade can only be maintained for so long. Within less than a year, the honeymoon phase of their relationship ended and Sally and my father were forced to confront the reality of their incompatibility as a couple. It was at this point that the monster within the stepmother emerged for all to witness. Sally was able, for the very first time, to allow her true colours to show; and this she revelled in.

Their arguments were fierce and devastating. Verbally and emotionally they tore each other to shreds. Shouting, slamming doors, sobbing late at night; such noises became a regular occurrence in the home. The only upside was that Sally, now focused on her miserable marriage, was slightly less focused on me and my brother.

Ours was not a happy home. If it wasn't all out war between Sally and my father, it was pained silences and an atmosphere of tension so thick you could cut it with a length of wire: dinners around the table with no one talking, silent trips in the car, family outings without laughter or smiles; a silent howling of pain, loneliness, and longing for love. The chill we felt in our bones.

Of course, it takes two to fight. It wasn't exclusively Sally's fault. My father was a troubled man, an alcoholic, a psychological wreck. He contributed in his own way to the domestic misery: by being self-absorbed, emotionally absent, and unable to fully embrace the roles of husband and father.

Meanwhile, we continued to see our mother every fortnight and most school holidays. These periods away, brief though they were, provided a welcome break from the drama and misery of life back home.

One school holiday period, my mother dragged us along to a week-long Tibetan Buddhist retreat. A less than formal event, it was held at Jennifer and Arnold's house, with half of the retreatants accommodated indoors and the other half forced to camp outside in tents and swags.

In an attempt to give the place a Tibetan Buddhist flavour, Jennifer and Arnold, with the help of their children, decorated the property with multiple threads of Tibetan prayer flags. They hung above us like Christmas lights: between the tops of trees, between the rooves of buildings, criss-crossing here and there in confusing and chaotic ways. They would flap like tiny birds whenever the breeze picked up, filling the environment with colour, movement and sound.

They kept coming loose, falling to the ground and causing much annoyance—and some degree of hazard—to both people and animals. Jennifer and Arnold kept goats for milking and at one point a goat showed up at the house, bleating wildly, a string of prayer flags tangled around its neck. The poor creature almost died from asphyxiation.

Though organised and facilitated by Jennifer and Arnold, the retreat was led by Rinpoche. For years he'd been their teacher, and now he was my mother's as well. As a boy of seven, the Chinese invaded his country of Tibet and he was forced to flee with his family to India. Having finally settled in Australia, he'd since acquired an appreciable amount of real estate and hundreds of devoted students, most of them white, middle-aged women, all of them seeking spiritual guidance and the promise of enlightenment.

He was, in the view of those who followed him, not just a man but a living God. A fully enlightened being. A Buddha. No longer caught up in the samsaric cycle of death and rebirth, he had chosen to incarnate in the form of a flesh-and-blood man in order to help others achieve liberation from suffering—just as he'd been doing for hundreds if not thousands of years—and would continue to do so until all sentient beings were free.

As a child, I'd watched *The Way of the Dragon* multiple times and had come to admire Bruce Lee. Like many children obsessed with Lee and the desire to be a martial arts master, my brother and I made nunchakus, staffs, and would stage fights between each other and our friends. We would try to channel Lee: his energy, charisma, strength and poise. It was our way of trying to be gods. And so, naturally, the chance to meet a living God I faced with great anticipation.

The scene I still recall clearly. It was mid-morning, and we'd just arrived at the retreat after a long drive from the airport. My mother was off somewhere, probably mingling with the other retreatants. It was just me and my brother in the room, seated lazily on the couch. The shoelaces of our sneakers were undone and our backpacks lay crumpled on the floor in front of us. We were bored, hungry, worn out.

A moment later Jennifer entered the room, smiling. After asking us about our trip, she said, "You must meet Rinpoche. He's such a nice man."

We waited in silence while she went to fetch him. It seemed to take an unusually long time. As the minutes passed, I began to wonder if she'd forgotten about us entirely.

Suddenly the door swung open and there stood Rinpoche accompanied by Jennifer.

If this was Buddha, I was greatly disappointed. He forced a smile as he shook our hands. He looked tired and unwell, his skin pasty and covered in blotches. Though he wore a shiny, decorative robe that flowed all the way down to his feet, it looked incongruous, almost as if it were a costume and he an actor in a cheap play.

He turned to Jennifer. "Jen, would you mind going to my room and grabbing some Easter eggs for the boys?"

She looked concerned. "You keep giving them away, Rinpoche. If you keep this up, there'll be none left for you."

"They're my last two eggs but they boys can have them." He patted his belly, pushing it out a little to make himself appear fatter. "I've been eating too much chocolate anyway. They'd be doing me a favour."

"Okay, Rinpoche. Right away."

With Jennifer out of the room to fetch the chocolate eggs, Rinpoche asked me and my brother if we liked watching WWF. He said he'd brought along some Hulk Hogan videos that, if we wanted, we could borrow.

When she returned, Jennifer handed Rinpoche the two Easter eggs. They were medium-sized and wrapped in purple foil. One he gave to my brother, the other to me. I thanked him, placing it in my pocket for later.

My brother had partially unwrapped his egg and was looking at it strangely, sniffing it, poking it, deciding whether or not to eat the suspicious candy; it was dark chocolate, which he didn't like, and the thing looked old, not quite fresh.

Jennifer asked Rinpoche if he wanted tea. Sounding irritated, he said he didn't, adding that he was tired and wanted to go to his room.

After they'd left, I took the egg out of my pocket and held it for a long time, contemplating its significance. Was it right to accept chocolate from the Buddha, I wondered? Was this a test, and, if so, had I already failed?

To my surprise, the retreat passed quickly. While the adults were inside meditating, chanting in Tibetan, and hanging on Rinpoche's every word, we children found plenty to do outdoors. My brother and I, plus Jennifer and Arnold's son, Luke, along with several other boys, spent our time playing ninjas in the forest, swinging over the dam on a home-made flying fox, and building slingshots and other weapons which we then used for target practice.

There were girls too, but they mainly kept to themselves. I developed a crush on a girl my age. She was mixed-race, her father Sikkimese and her mother Caucasian. I was captivated by her bronze skin and shiny, jet-black hair. She'd dyed her fringe purple and it looked pretty, slightly punk.

I discovered she liked the *Red Hot Chilli Peppers*, enjoyed skateboarding, and that she attended a school right in the heart of the city. Unlike me, she was cool. She knew how to engage in banter and was well on her way to mastering the art of witticism. In the social skills department, I was years behind, a mere Neanderthal by comparison.

When she made the comment we were standing on the balcony, right below Rinpoche's bedroom. Bolted vertically to the wall in front of us was a thick plastic pipe. Suddenly we heard the toilet above us flush and for a moment or two the pipe vibrated, heavy with shit, piss, and toilet water.

I looked at her. She looked at me. An impish grin appeared on her face. "I think we just witnessed a miracle," she said.

"A miracle, really?"

Her grin widened. "A holy shit kind of miracle."

19

THE PASTOR OF THE church was named Simon and the members of his congregation addressed him on a first name basis, this being in keeping with the church's image as a relaxed, youth-focused, egalitarian community.

One Sunday following the service, as I was getting ready to head out the door, Simon approached me with the suggestion that we meet for coffee sometime in order to "get to know each other better."

I was of course aware of his actual intention: he wanted to set me straight about Jesus, to evangelise, for I still harboured obvious doubts about Christianity and this was known to many within the church. What good is a pastor, after all, if he can't convert at least a few lost souls to the one true faith?

Some people radiate a certain unique energy that makes them fascinating creatures to observe, and this is how I'd come to think of Simon. Up close he looked even taller and ganglier. Whiter, too. More skeleton than flesh. He reminded me of a certain front man from a well-known Australian pub rock band.

We met a few days later at a café on the outskirts of town, where his pretty, twenty-one-year-old daughter worked as a barista. It was by no means the fanciest looking establishment—the building itself was a weatherboard townhouse that had since been converted into a café, and the renovations looked odd—yet their coffee, I'd been told, was the finest in town.

Simon's arrival was punctual. He was dressed the same way he dressed for church—in skinny jeans and a tight, black sweater—except on this occasion he also wore a scarf. His daughter was behind the counter and it was she who served us our coffees, he ordering a straight white and I a cappuccino. He insisted on paying for mine, though this made me a little uncomfortable; pastors, the honest ones at least, aren't exactly wealthy.

We decided to sit outside in the courtyard. Ours was the only occupied table; the rest of the customers were inside. He asked me about my background and what factors had brought me to church. I told him I was divorced, single, had a son. I explained that my motive for going to church was driven by a desire to improve my life and to see if Christianity had the answers I was seeking.

"So you're a seeker then?" he asked.

I tried the coffee. It tasted good: a strong, rich brew. "Yes, which places me in a bit of a strange position, I suppose."

He leaned forward, curious. "How do you mean?"

"I mean that most of the people you speak to are probably true believers."

He cocked his head, thinking. "No, not always. Faith is an ongoing issue, even among the faithful. Of course, as Christians we are supported in our faith by the Holy Spirit."

"I'm confused by the notion of the Holy Spirit," I admitted.

"Ours is a triune God: Father, Son and Holy Spirit. The Holy Spirit is the breath of God. It's through the Holy Spirit that God works miracles and makes his presence known in the world. If you haven't yet received the gift of the Holy Spirit—as in your case—you're not truly living a Christ-filled life."

To hear Simon say that I lacked the Holy Spirit made me feel unworthy and unfairly judged; I wanted him to think well of me, to count me as part of his congregation.

Just then an elderly lady entered the courtyard accompanied by a white Scottish terrier on a leash. She chose a table a few meters away, sat down, and began to read the paper and drink her coffee. The terrier took a spot directly at her feet, its ears pointed upward in alertness.

"Once you're filled with the Holy Spirit," continued Simon, "anything is possible. God becomes an enduring presence in your life. Miracles happen: people are healed, sometimes they talk in tongues, and the demonic influence is weakened."

His last point I was troubled by. The demonic, really? "How do you define the demonic?" I asked.

"In relation to Satan, of course. Whereas God, in the form of the Holy Spirit, brings people, communities and families together, Satan isolates and scatters. In fact, 'diablo' means 'the one who divides.' If we look closely enough, we can see these two principals at work in the world: God on one side, His adversary on the other."

I felt a pair of eyes boring into the side of my head, so immediately turned. It was the old lady. She was staring at us, her expression one of intense irritation.

She waited a few seconds before speaking, all the while continuing to stare. "I came here for a moment's peace, not to hear a conversation about religious mumbo-jumbo."

Simon addressed the old lady with a calm smile. "I'm a pastor. I apologise for the 'religious mumbo-jumbo' as you call it, but it's my job to spread the good news."

"This is a café. How about you take your job elsewhere and leave me in peace?"

I remained mute. I didn't want to get involved and I was curious to see how Simon would handle the confrontation.

He stood up, raising his hands in mock surrender. "We'll leave you in peace, madam. And I'll keep you and your family in my prayers."

"Fuck off," she snarled. "Shove your prayers up your ass. I don't need them."

Her dog, formerly quiet, stood up and started growling, its lips pulled back and sharp teeth exposed. Ironically, almost comically, the thing looked demoniacally possessed.

I followed Simon inside. As soon as we were re-seated, I noticed he was pale in the face, shaken by the incident yet trying his best to maintain his composure.

"Are you okay?" I asked.

He emitted a polite laugh. "I'm fine. This sort of thing happens more than you'd think. You'd be surprised how hostile people can get when the 'G' or 'J' word is mentioned."

"Are you really going to pray for her?"

"Absolutely. Jesus forgives. And he saves. She deserves God's love just as much as anyone else."

"Don't forget to pray for her dog too," I joked. "That thing was evil-looking."

He shrugged, finding no humour in the comment. "God works in mysterious ways. So too does the devil."

"You're saying her dog was demonically possessed? And the old lady? Her too?"

"I don't discount it as a possibility. We're living at a time when the forces of darkness are very close indeed."

"You know, I read a book recently about Satanism and Hollywood. It was written by a guy named Jasun Horsley. He argues that movies are elaborate occult rituals designed to capture our attention and shape our psyches. Weird book, but I have to say he makes a strong case."

"Interesting. I haven't read it but I'd agree with the author: much of what we call 'popular culture' is the demonic plain and simple. Even many of our most valued institutions—government, education, marriage, family, economy—have been infiltrated and manipulated by the dark powers.

Satan uses whatever he can, however he can, to lead people astray. He wants humanity to dwell in darkness and he's doing a very good job of it."

"That's both frightening and bleak," I said. "If this world belongs to Satan, then what hope is there for humanity?"

"You're looking at it from the wrong perspective, Chuck. The darkness we see in the world is merely that: darkness. It's a lie, a deception, perpetrated by Satan. He has no ultimate authority. He thinks he does but he doesn't. Jesus is Lord and salvation is to be found through him."

———

I went to bed early that night but sleep seemed impossible; all I could do was toss and turn. Finally giving up, I switched on the light. For a long time I lay there staring up at the water-stained ceiling, my mind burdened with existential dread and thoughts about my unsettling conversation with Simon.

Simon believed in Satan just as strongly as he believed in God. Although I wasn't onboard with the Christian definition of Satan as a supernatural being or entity, the notion of Satan as an objective source of evil—as that which sought to directly oppose human happiness and well-being—was, in my mind, impossible to refute.

Simon had spoken about Satan's influence in a collective sense; in relation to pop culture and so on. But what about Satan's influence on an individual level?

Was my own life evidence of the satanic? I wasn't a Christian and knew nothing of the Holy Spirit and its protective qualities. Presumably, then, from a Christian point of view, I was open to Satan's influence.

Satan cursed people, and my life at this moment seemed very much like a curse. I was divorced, a single father, and my career as a writer—if indeed you could call it a career—had reached an impasse. Nothing in my life was working, let alone blossoming. Everything was decaying, winding down, going nowhere. At some point I'd hit a dead end. Only instead of finding a way forward, I'd remained stationary, stuck.

I had always believed that happiness could be found by means of human connection. Yet through no obvious fault of my own, my existence had become the very definition of lonely. I barely got to see my son or play much of a role in his life. As for a romantic partner, I had none. I had a date with Stephanie, true, but I saw little hope of our forming a relationship.

For the first time in my life, I closed my eyes and prayed to God. Nothing happened. There was no feeling of peace or love, no presence of the divine. Though sleep finally came.

20

THAT DAY I TOOK my son to the beach.

The tide was out as far as it could go, an endless expanse of corrugated yellow sand between us and the glistening blue water. I located a shady spot under a thicket of tea trees and here we sat down to build sandcastles.

My son had never built a sandcastle before so I showed him how it was done: scoop the sand into the bucket, pack it down tight, then invert the bucket and voila—you have a sand tower.

After I'd finished erecting tower number three and was in the process of refilling the bucket, it occurred to my son that, rather than witness his father build a sandcastle, it was much more amusing to see the thing flattened.

"Don't," I almost shouted. "There's no point if you're going to stomp on it."

"Sorry, dad."

"That's okay," I sighed.

Bored, he picked up a stick, using it to dig holes in the sand. Finally tired of the stick, he threw it away, then started collecting shiny pebbles. As always, I kept him in my peripheral vision. The kid was a fast runner, capable of disappearing in a split second, especially when he had it in his mind that chasing seagulls was a good idea.

Disappointed, I packed away the bucket and spade. As children, my brother and I excelled at building sandcastles. Ours were large and elaborate structures, complete with turreted walls, bridges, moats and other features. Eventually the tide would wash them away, but to destroy them ourselves was out of the question, such was the pride we took in our work.

As we got older, other beach activities followed: flying kites, snorkelling, bodyboarding. Perving on girls came later. I was fifteen when I saw my first pair of tits at the beach. She was lying on her back on a brightly coloured beach towel, sunbathing; a well-built, blonde-haired girl about the same age as me. She'd removed her bikini top but still had on her bikini briefs. Her tits were huge: two white mounds with cherries in the middle, flattened a little under their own weight.

They were magical, glorious, the greatest things I'd ever seen. The girl caught me staring but didn't seem to care, although she giggled when she noticed that my adolescent boner was making a tent of my swimming trunks. Embarrassed, I ran straight into the sea, crashing among the waves. I remained in the water a long time, not coming out till I was absolutely certain that my dick was soft again and no longer misbehaving.

I pushed the memory away, bringing my full attention back to my son. He was standing on the edge of a puddle in the sand, a smile on his face, throwing into the water the rocks he'd collected. They splashed loudly, sending droplets flying in all directions.

I wanted to tell him to stop but didn't have the heart to say it. Already his sneakers were damp, and I knew it was just a matter of time before his pants and top would be damp as well, at which point I'd have to get him changed. Oh well, I thought, the kid deserves to have some fun. Let him.

His mother and I were concerned he had autism. We'd noticed that, even as an infant, he was different, unique. Compared to other children his age, he was less expressive, less in tune with his environment, less able to communicate and engage socially. I was worried he might be slow, incapable of attending a normal school and having a normal life. Yet my immediate concern was for his safety. He operated on his own wavelength, existed in his own little world, and there loomed the ever-present danger that he might simply wander off and go missing.

Gazing out at the horizon, I noticed two portly figures lumbering along the shoreline. The figure in front was slightly taller and fatter than the figure dawdling behind. From this distance—and because of the peculiar angle of the sun—they looked less like people and more like great beasts migrating across a barren landscape. As they drew closer, it became apparent that the taller figure was Brian and the shorter figure his stepdaughter, Gemma.

I waved, and a moment later they came over. Brian was dressed in striped boardshorts and thongs, and atop his head, tilted slightly to the side, sat a wide-brimmed straw hat. Gemma, though hatless, was covered from head to toe in a thick coating of sunscreen. Brian, when he'd applied it, must've used a whole bottle and then some.

They sat down beside me. Brian removed his hat, then ran a hand through his thinning hair. "Lovely day," he remarked, gesturing towards a vista of gentle blue water, azure sky and silvery cumulus.

"Funny running into you here," I said.

"It was Gemma's idea that we visit the beach." Laughing, he added, "She's the boss and I'm her butler. Isn't that right, Gemma?"

Gemma said nothing; the comment didn't register. She extended an index finger, placed it on her chin, then moved it down to her chest. It took me a moment to recognise that she was using sign language.

"It means she's thirsty," said Brian. "Say, would you happen to have any water on you, Chuck?"

"Sure thing," I replied.

My son's mother had packed him a bag containing a bottle of water and a few snacks. I unzipped it, then handed the bottle of water to Gemma. She guzzled it down in a matter of seconds, leaving behind not a single drop.

"Thanks, Chuck," said Brian. "You're a life saver. Gemma is one thirsty animal. She has a heck of an appetite too. You should see her consume a piece of cake. Boy she loves cake!"

"I don't doubt it."

My son by this stage had grown bored throwing pebbles. He wandered over, sat down on my lap, his curly hair rubbing against my chin.

"Lovely boy you have there," said Brian. "I remember when Gemma was that age. I tried to read her stories but she could never understand them, so I gave up. Television, though, she enjoyed. Still does. *Sesame Street*, *Playschool*: all the kids' shows. She loves 'em."

Gemma handed me the empty bottle and I placed it back inside my son's bag. As I was drawing the zip closed, I noticed something at the bottom of the bag that earlier I'd missed: a shiny, white business card.

I fished it out, turned it over in my hand. It belonged to a real estate agent named Catherine Roberts, a serious-looking woman with straight black hair. Beneath her name was the title of Property Sales Representative.

It was obvious that my son had acquired the card from his mother, claiming it as a "toy," as he was known to do with all sorts of random objects.

"Thinking of buying a house?" asked Brian.

"As someone who makes their living from writing, I already own several properties," I joked. "Would I really want another?"

Brain squinted in confusion.

"I was kidding. I'm far too poor to buy a house."

"Oh right. Maybe one day. When you write a bestseller."

"Maybe."

The significance of the card I recognised straight away. My ex-wife, who despised Tasmania on account of its cold climate, had several times hinted at the idea of selling her house and moving to Queensland. It was clear what was happening:

lately she'd been meeting with real estate agents to have her property valued. Already she was getting the ball rolling on the process of moving interstate.

I wouldn't have been worried were it not for the fact that she had full custody of our son. Legally she had the freedom to move wherever she liked and to take our son with her, and there was not a damn thing I could do to stop her.

I explained the whole dismal situation to Brian. He was good about it. He listened closely, not once interrupting.

He asked, "If she ends up moving, are you prepared to move too?"

Up till this moment, I hadn't given the question much thought. I shrugged and said, "I'll move for my son, if that's what I have to do."

"Good for you, Chuck. That boy of yours needs a father in his life, and I can see you're doing a good job with him."

"Thanks. Same with you and Gemma."

"Just doing my God-given duty."

"Speaking of God," I asked, "lately I've been pondering a theological matter that I was hoping you could clarify."

"Sure. You know I'm always happy to help when it's a question about the Lord."

Just then Gemma emitted a noise similar to that of an animal in distress. It reminded me of the hee-haw of a donkey. Startled, I involuntarily titled my head back. My son was asleep in my arms; he didn't stir.

"It's one of the ways she communicates," explained Brian.

"Do the noises differ depending on what's she saying?"

"Not really. Although she does get very vocal whenever the Lord is mentioned. She loves the Lord, Gemma does. She may be mute and slow but she's filled with the Holy Spirit. Aren't you, Gemma?"

Again she hee-hawed, this time quieter, as if in affirmation.

"What's your question?" asked Brian.

"The God you believe in is a loving God who wants the best for humanity, right? Who wants to see each human being thrive?"

"Of course."

"Then why do I see so much brokenness in the world? There are families torn apart. Husbands separated from wives. Children separated from parents. People alone, depressed, isolated. I mean, look at the two of us: you're divorced from your wife; I'm divorced from mine. You still see your stepdaughter, but this doesn't change the fact that you're a single guy without a family. The same goes for me. We're only getting older too. I'm sorry to say, but we're fucked.

"Of course, when you think about it, we're better off than most. It's worse for the children. There are children born into families that are already broken; children who, from the very beginning, don't have a chance at happiness. And what about the children born sick and crippled? What about the ones who die in horrible accidents? Surely a loving God would never allow such things."

Brian looked shocked, his mouth agape. It was insensitive of me to openly criticise his God. But I was on a roll now. I couldn't stop. Besides, it felt good to shake my fist at the sky and to do so in the company of a true believer.

"If there's a God, Brian, he's not the God of the Bible. He doesn't care about us as individuals. He's entirely indifferent to our suffering. In fact, I had a dream recently in which I met Bukowski..."

"—Bukowski? Who's he?"

"Charles Bukowski, the famous author."

"Oh."

"Anyway, I met Bukowski and he described God as a kind of scientist and each human life an experiment. Think about it: you're an experiment. I'm an experiment. My son is an experiment. Gemma is an experiment. It's all random, really. It's like when you plant some seeds in pots and they sprout into seedlings. Some grow tall. Some grow stunted. Some are affected by disease. Others are perfectly healthy. There's no justice or fairness to it; it's just science. Do you get the drift of what I'm saying? Maybe this is what Jesus meant when he explained to his disciples the Parable of the Sower."

"Watch it, Chuck. You're being blasphemous. This Bukowski fellow, how do you know he wasn't evil or possessed? How do you know you're not being misled by the devil?"

Just then Gemma became agitated, hee-hawing loudly, and in the process waking my son. Unable to calm her down, Brian took Gemma's hand and began to escort her in the direction of the parking lot.

"Anything I can do to help?" I asked.

As he was walking away, he turned and said, "Gemma loves the Lord. How could you upset her, Chuck? How could you say those things about the Lord?"

21

ONE SCHOOL HOLIDAY PERIOD when I was 15-years-old, my brother and I made the usual trip to visit our mother in rural Victoria. At the time she lived at a Buddhist retreat centre where she also worked as a caretaker. Left unsupervised for the duration of our stay, my brother and I spent the majority of our time indoors, watching movies, playing video games, eating junk food, and fighting like a couple of house cats.

The holidays we spent with our mother always passed quickly. On the final day of our stay, we'd get up early and she'd drive us to the bus depot in the city. Our coach was number 37 and the drivers all looked the same: portly guys with thinning grey hair, dressed in white shirts and black pants. Men with names like "Gordon" and "Fred." Clones devoid of personality. Rarely did they speak, not once did they complain. They simply did their job. They drove the bus.

After handing our bags to the driver to place in the luggage compartment, we'd each give our mother a hug and climb aboard the coach, our faces forlorn. I didn't want to go home. Neither did my brother. I felt like an inmate facing the death penalty, a knot of tension at the base of my guts. Dad, since his divorce from Sally, had taken up drinking, and life with him was agony. And the thought of having to go back to school made everything that much worse.

The trip home took around 24 hours and was boring as hell. Uncomfortable, too. The bus didn't stop very often. When it did stop, it would be at a service station or a general store in some crappy little town in the middle of nowhere.

The toilets at those places were rarely clean. I remember once going inside because I badly needed to take a piss, and nearly stepping on a giant, steaming turd; some weirdo had taken a shit right there on the floor, the thing strategically placed to ruin someone's day. A close shave indeed. I wondered about the fate of the next poor sucker who entered.

If we were lucky, the bus driver would put on a movie. In those days the standard was VHS and TVs were fairly small, especially the ones inside coaches. You'd be forced to strain your neck to catch a glimpse of the damn screen, and you could never quite hear the dialogue over the rumbling of the diesel engine.

Of course, you'd be lucky to get a good movie. On one bus trip, it was a movie about the Vietnam war. Violent as hell. American soldiers gunning down peasants in rice paddies and raping all the women. By the third rape scene, the driver finally realised it was inappropriate for younger viewers and switched it off. For years I had nightmares about the scenes in that movie.

I didn't sleep easily on the bus; it was far too uncomfortable. For the most of the journey I'd gaze out the window, taking in the scenery. Occasionally it'd be pretty, I'd spot a beautiful mountain or river. Mostly, though, it was endless paddocks and dry scrub. An empty wasteland.

Not that the emptiness bothered me. I recall pleasant moments spent on the bus in which, lulled into a state of relaxation by the rhythmic sound and motion of the vehicle, altered states of consciousness came easily to me. During these moments, my mind would take the form of a soaring bird and I would find myself reflecting on the purpose and meaning of life.

I thought a lot about the Buddhist notion of karma. I didn't like my life very much; therefore, to think that I was wholly responsible for the current state of my existence—that the sum of my actions and decisions in the past, including those taken in previous incarnations, had led me to become Chuck Valentine and to have the parents and siblings that I did—was enough to send me spiralling into an existential crisis.

———

This holiday period was different to those previous. On the final day, when it came time to leave, it was only my brother who boarded the bus. With my mother's encouragement, I'd chosen to stay behind. From that point on I was to live with her. My brother would continue living with our father.

At the Buddhist centre I was given my own room. It was cramped, with just enough space to fit a single bed, a desk, and a wardrobe for my clothes. There was little privacy, especially when the place filled up with guests. The walls were thin and many rooms neighboured mine. I heard it all: people fucking, sneezing, coughing, farting, arguing. I came to loathe those periods when there were guests and enjoy those periods when there weren't.

It was hardly a luxurious place to reside. To my great annoyance, the toilets and showers were located outside, in their own separate blocks. When I needed to take a piss in the middle of the night, I was forced to don a pair of slippers and brave the cold and the dark. This became a problem when, at the age of seventeen, I developed an inexplicable fear of the night time.

To gaze up at the stars in the dead of night—to see them spread out above me in all their majesty and power—was enough to induce in me a feeling of sheer terror, but also a deep sense of wonder and curiosity. I began to think deeply about the question of extra-terrestrial life. After reading several books on UFOs, I became convinced that malevolent alien beings were visiting earth and abducting humans.

I'm not sure what I hoped to gain by believing in aliens. Perhaps it's that I needed to somehow personify—give an image and label to—that which I took to be the presence of evil in the world. Maybe it was easier, less psychologically burdensome, to believe in grey-skinned demons from space than to accept that my life sucked and my parents didn't love me.

Such coping strategies, I later discovered, are typical of kids and adolescents trapped in abusive and broken homes. Whether it's achieved through an obsession with *Marvel* movies, fantasy novels and computer games, or, as in my case, via an insatiable appetite with the paranormal, the desire is the same: to escape into an alternate reality.

My mother, though I was her responsibility now, wasn't interested in raising me. She considered me a burden and my problems insignificant. Her duties as a caretaker, which included scrubbing toilets, cleaning rooms and fixing Rinpoche his meals, took precedence in her life over those of being a mother.

They worked her like a slave but she didn't seem to mind. From her perspective, serving Rinpoche and the Buddhist community was the height of honour and an effective way to generate positive karma. Once she'd generated enough positive karma, she believed, she'd either attain enlightenment or be reborn in the "pure realm."

She spoke a lot about the pure realm. I imagined it as a place of fluffy white clouds and levitating Buddhas; a kind of Eastern version of heaven. I imagined, too, that the spirit of Bruce Lee had been reborn there; that the guy was happy, that he practiced martial arts every day and lounged in hot mountain springs shrouded in mist, accompanied by cheerful monkey companions.

When the school term started, I had the option of either doing home-schooling or enrolling in the local high school. I chose the former. It suited my lazy, introverted nature.

The work was easy and there was little of it. A short writing exercise, a few maths problems, maybe a quiz or two and I was finished by the early afternoon, free to enjoy the rest of the day in leisure. My teachers—none of whom I met face-to-face—didn't demand much of me. Even my laziest efforts were rewarded with an "A."

Naturally, I became a layabout, a homebody, a good-for-nothing. When I wasn't studying, reading novels, or listening to music, I was whacking off to the images of naked women in the porn mags I hid beneath my mattress, fantasising about what it would be like to get with a girl.

Another pastime of mine—in which the devil or devils made effective use of my young, idle hands —was to explore those hidden and neglected parts of the Buddhist centre.

The place was over half-a-century old and most of its buildings were heavily decayed and badly in need of maintenance. Previously it had served as a rehab centre, and before that a mental health facility. Fittingly, there was little rhyme or reason to its layout; it felt random, disorganised, as though designed by a kid with a Lego set.

One of the caretakers, a guy in his sixties named Colin, had been given the excruciating task of repainting all of the exterior and interior walls. His efforts were futile; no matter how many coats of paint he applied, no matter how skilfully he worked his brush, the place still resembled a junkyard.

I did what one would normally do in a junkyard: I explored its many nooks and crannies; I scavenged among the trash, debris and decay. After a group cleared out—normally they stayed no longer than a week or two—I'd go from room to room, checking to see if anything of interest had been left behind by any of the guests.

Some of my more noteworthy finds included a Gameboy, a compendium of women's sexual fantasies, and a Stretch Armstrong doll. All of these items I kept.

There were also items I didn't keep. These include a pack of adult diapers, a caramel toupee, two pairs of shit-stained underwear, and—most memorable of all—the dildo wrapped in cloth I found tucked away at the back of a drawer.

An eight-inch monstrosity, it was purple, veiny, made of latex, and when I picked it up by the balls it jiggled. I was both fascinated and disturbed by its sheer length and girth.

For the first time in my life, I felt deeply flawed and inadequate. If this was the size a dick ought to be, what was I to do about mine? Mine was nothing more than a baby dick, a pencil pecker.

I had a healthy body. I wasn't exactly ugly. Yet I possessed one major flaw: my dick was too small. With it I could never hope to fully please a woman. The creator—if he existed—had played a cruel joke on me.

I'll never forget the dildo; it haunts me still. It was just a hunk of latex, an implement designed to ease the frustration of horny men and women; and yet, after seeing the thing, I was never the same again. It set me on a path of self-discovery, a spiritual quest, a search for truth.

Buddhism, as a religion, interested me very little. It involved sitting cross-legged for long periods of time, ringing bells, beating drums, and chanting in Tibetan, a language obscure and difficulty to pronounce. Plus, to be a really good Buddhist, you had to kiss Rinpoche's ass by offering him cups of tea in fancy mugs and laughing at all of his bad jokes.

Yet I remained fascinated by alleged accounts of mind-over-matter performed by Eastern yogis. Feats such as raising their body temperature enough to melt the snow around them. Feats that could only be achieved after years of disciplining the mind and body through meditation, yoga, fasting and prayer.

I'd heard stories of yogis accomplishing wonders with their dicks, such as pulling trucks and lifting heavy weights. I hadn't heard of them making their dicks bigger, but I felt this might be possible. With this goal in mind—and also because I wanted to be stronger, more powerful—I took up a regular meditation practice. I'd become a kind of yogi, I decided.

It wasn't long before my mother noticed. It filled her with pride to see her son meditate; to know that he, as far as she could tell, was on his way to becoming a Buddhist. Eventually she suggested I have a private meeting with Rinpoche.

22

IT WAS SEVERAL WEEKS before I heard from Stephanie with an invitation to meet up. Her text message came as a surprise to me; I thought she'd lost interest after our last dismal date and wasn't expecting to hear from her at all. To my further surprise, she suggested not that we meet for dinner but that we spend the weekend together at a holiday cabin in the Golden Valley.

She told me she'd booked the place about a month in advance with the intention of enjoying a weekend alone of R&R. After then deciding she wished to have some company after all, it occurred to her—apparently on the spur of the moment—to invite me along.

She apologised for failing to contact me earlier, saying she'd been busy, and promised that if I joined her on this trip she'd "make it up to me." It would be just the two of us; her daughter was to stay with grandparents.

I accepted without giving it much thought. Spending the weekend alone with her implied getting laid, an opportunity I couldn't turn down.

The more I thought about it, however, the more I began to question her motive for inviting me. It didn't make sense.

Why ignore a guy for three weeks, then, out of the blue, invite him to join you on a weekend trip? The only explanation I could think of is that she desired a fling, not a serious relationship, and that I happened to be her most convenient option. We'd meet up, have sex. And maybe—if she didn't think I was terrible in bed—we'd see each other again.

Although ideally I wanted a girlfriend, I was happy to settle for a friend-with-benefits or simply a one-night stand. I hadn't been laid in months, and beggars, as they say, can't be choosers.

Stephanie suggested that we take separate cars and that I meet her at the cabin on the Saturday morning. This I preferred as opposed to sharing a vehicle. Car trips with woman are never much fun. I don't like to make small talk while I'm driving; I prefer to listen to music and focus on the road in front of me and the grip of the steering wheel. There's a peace that can be found on the open road when it's just you and no one else. It's lonely, sure, but there's comfort in the loneliness if you know how to find it.

I spent the morning getting ready: showering, shaving, packaging my bag, polishing my shoes, making sure I looked half-decent. I dressed in khaki pants and a denim shirt and wore my best leather belt. Condoms, luckily, I didn't need to buy; I still had some left over from when Lucy and I were dating.

It felt a little strange to bring along condoms that I'd originally purchased to fuck another woman. I had to remind myself that they were only latex sheaths wrapped in foil. There was nothing special about them, nothing sentimental. To hell with Lucy anyway: she hadn't been good to me and I'd stopped missing her a long time ago.

Of course, there was a possibility that Stephanie would already have condoms. I wasn't counting on it, though; she struck me as too much of a lady for that. Only sluts supplied their own. Then again, maybe she was a slut. She'd invited me to spend the weekend with her and we barely knew each other. Hardly the behaviour of a shy, sexually-reserved lady.

By the time I climbed into my car and hit the road, it was already nine o'clock. It was perfect rainbow weather, a combination of sunny and rainy. For the first hour or so, I simply took in the scenery; the rolling greens fields, the farmhouses, the trees.

Growing bored, I reached into the glove compartment and removed the bundle of albums I'd placed there. I started with Warren Zevon's *Excitable Boy*, by far his best album in terms of sheer number of hits.

I've long been a fan of Zevon. His songs are catchy, original, yet I'd also come to appreciate the dark humour and philosophical musings contained in his lyrics. In several of his songs about woman and relationships, I detected a certain masculine attitude that could be summed up as lovingly not giving a fuck.

This attitude I needed to adopt myself. In relationships I had a tendency to put myself second, focusing all of my energies on making the other person happy while neglecting to think about myself and my own needs.

In my marriage, I'd cared so much, given so much, that I'd reduced myself to an empty vessel, a nobody, a loser. My then wife, no longer able to recognise in me the man whom she'd married, quickly lost all attraction and respect for me. A similar dynamic had played itself out in my relationship with Lucy.

I'd since made a promise to myself that if I happened to get into another relationship, I'd handle things differently. This time I'd refuse to give her everything. No woman, no matter how desirable, was worth that kind of sacrifice. I reminded myself to keep this in mind when interacting with Stephanie.

By the time I was part-way through track six of Zevon's *Bad Luck Streak in Dancing School*, I'd reached the town of Deloraine. I parked on the main street, opposite a strip of cafes. I was hungry and needed to empty my bladder. The latter I took care of first; there was a public toilet just down the road.

At a cafe named the *Able Inn*, I ordered a coffee and a ham and cheese sandwich from a tall proprietor with bushy eyebrows and a prominent Adams apple. I scoffed down the sandwich outside where I stood, my hunger overriding my sense of social grace.

I figured it would do me good to wander around for a bit, get some exercise and freshen up before completing the final leg of my journey. Plus, I was at least half-an-hour early, and to arrive at the cabin before the appointed time would signify desperation on my part. So, with hot coffee in hand, I wandered down to the nearby park.

As children, my brother and I had played here many times, drawn to its preserved steam train that sat in a small fenced area at the very periphery of the park. The driver's compartment was accessible via a small ladder. You could climb inside and pretend you were driving it.

The train still stood, though it had since been repainted in rainbow colours. Now it looked flashy, ridiculous, like a float out of a gay pride parade. I could only conclude that some LGBTQ activist member of the local council was responsible for this absurdity. Probably some fat, miserable lesbian with purple hair and sagging tits.

I found a bench in the shade and sat down. The park was all but empty, save for a heavily stooped old lady walking a corgi on a leash and a mother and her two young children feeding ducks at the riverbank. Overall the place had changed very little since I'd been here as a child decades ago.

I found myself recalling a memory from long ago of when my brother and I had stood at the riverbank as two little boys, captivated by the sight of the brown, fast-flowing water. Days of unending rain had caused the river to rise dramatically and our mother had brought us along to witness the spectacle.

Like most children, I had a strong curiosity with regard to animals; and in this instance my mind was dominated by a single thought: were there fish in the river, and if so, how big did they grow?

The thought was interrupted by a meaty slapping sound, as of something wet and soft making contact with something hard. When I looked down and saw it, my reaction was one of shock, then disbelief, then delight. From out of the fast-flowing water, a full-grown trout—easily some thirty inches long—had leapt and landed right at my feet.

"A fish! A fish!" I yelled, looking over at my mother. "I wanted a fish, mum, and I got one."

The fish was flopping around wildly on the rocks, its pink gills pumping spasmodically. Its efforts to return to its habitat were futile: one flop would carry it closer to the water, the next would carry it further away. It was pure instinct, pure muscle. A creature without mind or intelligence.

"Can we take it home?" I asked.

My mother, the Buddhist, had her doubts. The killing of animals and insects she objected to, though in the case of fish for eating she was known to make a partial exception, occasionally permitting my half-sister Noele to catch trout from local mountain streams by tickling them into a trance.

Just then my brother started crying. "Leave it alone," he protested, protectively placing himself between us and the fish.

I couldn't believe it. My brother was supposed to be the tough one, yet here he was crying over a damn fish. Deep down he was more of a sissy than I was.

His tears were enough to convince my mother that the fish was not to be harmed. I was devastated. My brother was elated. My mother cheered and gave him a clap as he picked it up in both hands, all slippery and writhing, and tossed it back into the river.

I never quite got over it. It was my fish, and yet it had been stolen from me, along with the victory and magic of the moment. What was rightfully mine my brother took, a dynamic that would continue as we got older.

I stood up, stretched, yawned. I finished what remained of my coffee, then tossed the paper cup in the bin. It was time to hit the road, but first there was something I needed to buy: alcohol.

Although I'd more or less given up alcohol, I felt it was necessary on this occasion: without a drink or two in my belly, I was unlikely to possess the gumption required to make a move on Stephanie, should the opportunity present itself.

There was a bottle shop over the road. From here I purchased a bottle of Moscato and a six-pack of apple cider. Then I climbed into my car and drove.

WHEN I PULLED UP at the cottage, Stephanie was seated on a reclining chair on the veranda drinking a glass of red wine and reading a copy of *Women's Lifestyle*. Dressed in hiking boots, jeans, and a woollen sweater, she looked the very definition of a single mother on a weekend holiday. Though outwardly she appeared relaxed, I could sense she wasn't entirely at ease.

"Glad you made it," she said, placing the magazine on the table in front of her. "How did you go finding the place?"

"Easy. I used to live around these parts. Most of the roads I'm familiar with."

She stood up, gazing out at the rolling green pastures peppered with native flowers and distant mountains. She inhaled deeply as if to sample the air. "So peaceful out here, wouldn't you agree?"

I said nothing, merely smiled.

"You don't like it?" she asked.

"Of course I like it. What makes you think I don't?"

She laughed, shook her head. "I'm sorry. Old habits die hard. When I was married, David, my ex, used silence as a way to show his disapproval. It used to get on my nerves."

I hadn't been here long, hadn't known Stephanie long, and already she was bringing up baggage from the past. Had I made a mistake by coming here?

"Sounds like your husband was a pain in the ass," I replied.

She laughed. "Yes, he was."

I spent a moment unloading my bags from the car. The apple cider and Moscato I placed in the bar fridge in the kitchen. Once these matters were out of the way, Stephanie showed me around the cottage.

The cottage was one of five situated on a 40-acre block of privately owned bush and farmland. Each consisted of a bedroom with ensuite and a combined kitchen-living room. Sliding doors and large windows afforded impressive views of the surrounding countryside.

Being "eco-friendly," the cottage relied on solar power in addition to mains electricity for backup. Water was supplied by rainwater tanks and all the grey water was recycled. To my relief, the toilet was the conventional kind: flush as opposed to compost.

I was pleased with the fact that the bedroom featured a king size bed. As much as I enjoy sleeping next to a woman, I hate being cramped.

"What do you think?" asked Stephanie.

"I think it's a great little cottage and I'm glad you invited me along."

"Thanks for agreeing to join me."

Without speaking, she slipped out of her shoes and stretched out on the mattress on her back, her feet dangling over the edge. I did the same, and for a long time we lay side by side, our hands touching.

When I turned to look at her, her expression had changed to one of mischief. She reached across, placing a hand squarely on my crotch. In seconds I was hard, my cock straining uncomfortably against the front of my trousers.

I placed my mouth over hers and we kissed deeply, fondling each other with eager hands. We helped each other undress, leaving our clothes in piles on the bedroom floor, and she led me by the hand into the bathroom.

I turned on the shower, adjusting the taps to get the temperature just right. Once satisfied, we stepped inside, immersing our bodies in the hot water and steam.

"I find it's always best to take a shower first," she said, seductively working the soap over her firm breasts and between her legs.

We kissed some more. Then she knelt down, taking my cock in her mouth. She knew what she was doing, applying just the right amount of suction, her rhythm perfect. She stopped just before I came and we then dried off and went into the bedroom.

Stephanie, it turned out, had purchased a box of condoms for the occasion. Instead I wore one of my own, rolling it carefully over my cock to create the best seal possible; though eager to get started,

I'm not one to take any chances when it comes to STIs and pregnancy.

We didn't bother to draw the curtains. She came as I was taking her missionary, her legs spread wide, moaning "yes, yes, yes" as she spasmed in orgasm. She then changed position, lying on her chest with a cushion under her pelvis. Just before I came, she looked back with gritted teeth and said, "Fuck my pussy hard. Use me."

24

WE SPENT THE AFTERNOON strolling along the paths that criss-crossed the property, occasionally holding hands, now and then stopping to kiss and cuddle. Except for one other couple—an Indian man and white woman—we saw no one else. By the time we returned to the shack, it was early afternoon and we were hungry. A light drizzle was beginning to fall.

For lunch we cooked meat patties on the barbeque, which we ate between buns stuffed with lettuce, tomato, onion and lots of mayonnaise.

Feeling lazy and sleepy, we lounged on the veranda in deck chairs and drank. Far above us circled a wedge-tailed eagle, patiently hunting for prey. We watched it until it drifted away and vanished, a tiny speck absorbed by the infinite sky.

I felt relaxed, satisfied, at peace. My balls empty, my belly full. A happy animal.

Stephanie had by this stage downed three glasses of wine and was now on her fourth. The alcohol had rendered her giggly and uninhibited.

Her laughter sounded like a gentle breeze playing against wind chimes, pure and free but not without pain.

"What did you think of that couple?" she asked.

"They looked sweet together. The guy had a grin on his face. I imagine, like us, they're having a lot of sex."

She chuckled. "You imagine?"

"A figure of speech. I don't mean I'm *imagining* them having sex. That's something I wouldn't want to imagine."

With obvious facetiousness, she said, "What? Because he's Indian and she's white? Interracial sex gross you out, does it?"

"Ha-ha. No. Trying to make me sound like a racist. Very funny."

"You know, I once fucked an Indian guy."

The comment caught me off guard. Trying not to lose my composure, trying to pretend as though I didn't give a shit, I managed the best response that I could: "Really?"

"Yes, really. You're not the first guy I've fucked, you know."

"That can't be," I joked, pulling a face of mock surprise. "And all along I thought you were a virgin. So an Indian guy, eh? What was that like?"

She shrugged, looking despondent. "Actually not so great. I was twenty-one, backpacking through India. I needed someone to show me around and a place to stay. He wanted something in return, so I gave it to him."

In an attempt to change the topic and lighten the mood, I asked, "Do you think that couple's fucking right now? And if so, in what position?"

She laughed. "Of course they're fucking. He's doing her on the floor, wheel-barrow style."

"I reckon it's something more exotic. The clapper, maybe, or the boa constrictor. Or the dirty dog."

"Those are actual positions?"

I laughed. "Maybe. I don't know."

Just then Stephanie's phone rang, startling the both of us. She walked inside to take the call in privacy, sliding the door closed behind her.

I assumed it had something to do with her daughter. I remained seated, waiting for the conversation to end, catching the occasional word. Stephanie's voice was calm but very soon it became raised.

Feeling like an eavesdropper, I picked up my bottle of cider and started down the hill, putting some distance between myself and the cabin. I found a wattle tree, sat down beneath it, kept drinking.

Earlier, during my walk with Stephanie, I'd noticed something odd. She'd been acting hot and cold, sending mixed messages. One moment we'd be kissing passionately; the next moment I'd reach for her and instead of reciprocating she'd turn away. Her message was clear: you're bothering me a little; I need space.

The story about the Indian guy also struck me as weird. Not wanting to make a big deal out of it, I'd said little at the time. Her sexual history was her own business and it wasn't my place to pry or judge. Yet I couldn't help but wonder: had she actually been raped? Was she a victim of sexual trauma?

Women, I thought: such wonderful creatures. But at the same time so damaged, so tragic, so sad.

I waited a while longer before making my way back to the cabin. I found Stephanie in the bedroom, sat perched on the edge of the bed, hot tears streaming down her flushed cheeks. I sat down beside her, placing a comforting hand on her upper-back. So profound was the state of her anguish that she barely seemed to notice my presence.

"Something to do with Kate?" I asked.

I handed her two tissues. One she used to blow her nose; the other she used to dry her eyes.

"No, it's not Kate."

"Her father, then?"

She shook her head. "It's to do with someone else. A friend. I'd rather not talk about it."

"That's fine," I replied. "If or when you want to talk about it, let me know."

She nodded, then pulled back the covers and manoeuvred herself into bed. She lay there with her back turned to me, the blankets pulled up level with the top of her head. I drew the curtains and left, quietly closing the door behind me.

I took out my copy of John Fante's *Ask the Dust* and sat down in an armchair in the lounge room to read. I kept an ear tilted in the direction of the bedroom. I heard more crying, followed by sniffling, then complete silence. Soon I grew weary of reading, so put down my book, resting it on my lap.

The sun was setting over the distant hills, a melancholic explosion of pink and tangerine. Another day was dying. For the most part it had been a good day. I'd gotten laid. That was a win. I was worried about Stephanie, though. I worried not because she was suffering. I worried that she might be unstable, troubled. I worried for myself. I worried I'd gotten involved with a crazy woman. A liability.

On the couch nearby sat a folded cotton blanket. I leaned over and grabbed it, then pulled it over my body. Feeling warm and relaxed, I closed my eyes.

Very soon I drifted to the edge of sleep. What appeared was a kind of daydream, only much more vivid. I found myself in an ancient city in what looked like the Middle East. The earth was scorched and the buildings made of mud. Above hung a turquoise blue sky flecked with wisps of delicate white cloud.

Milling about were men and women dressed in long, flowing robes, some of them accompanied by livestock, others hawking items such as rugs and ceramics, others selling fruit and vegetables from stalls. Lots of conversation, activity, laughter. A marketplace, perhaps, though not the usual kind.

Opposite me was a low garden wall and upon it sat a young woman with curly dark hair and olive skin. She was beautiful: twinkling hazel eyes, delicate lips, her figure petite. She radiated kindness and playful humour.

I had a strong sense that the woman was real and not simply a figment of my imagination. Somewhere out there she existed in the world, though as of yet our paths hadn't crossed. One day, however, we'd meet; at which point we'd fall in love and eventually marry. She was to be my wife and I her husband; it was God's will.

What, then, was I doing with Stephanie, I wondered? I suddenly felt very bad. She was the wrong woman for me. We weren't meant to be together. By sleeping with her, by giving into my lust, I'd committed a sin, gone against my fate, and for this I'd be forced to pay a price.

All of a sudden I was roused to full consciousness by the sight of bright headlights flashing through the window. It was now dark outside, and, foolish me, I'd forgotten to draw the curtains before nodding off to sleep.

I jumped out of the chair and sprang to my feet, throwing the blanket to the side. I approached the window and peered out, squinting against the brightness. The vehicle was a white 4WD Pajero. My first thought is that a newly-arrived guest had come to our cabin thinking it was theirs, in which case they'd soon realise their mistake and be gone.

The vehicle parked, and with engine still running and headlights still blazing, the driver disembarked. He was tall, auburn-haired, muscular and looked to be in his early-to-mid-twenties. Quite a strapping lad. His attire was that of a tradesman: lace-up boots, cargo pants, and a reflective yellow vest.

Probably a construction worker, I thought. Maybe there's been an emergency and he's here to alert us?

He was a man on a mission, his expression serious and focused. He mounted the steps and crossed the veranda in quick, powerful strides; and in seconds he was standing at the door, pounding on it with his fist.

Realising I'd forgotten to turn on the light, I reached across and flicked the switch, then slid open the door. I shivered as I felt cool air rush in.

"Is there a problem?" I inquired.

He glowered at me; about him was an aura of barely suppressed anger. "Is Stephanie here?"

"Yes. Why do you ask?"

What happened next was very sudden. The man came at me, fists blazing. I felt his knuckles connect with my jaw and nose. Bones crunched. Blood gushed from my nostrils, dripping down my chin and covering the front of my shirt. The next punch was harder, knocking me to the floor. I lay there wincing in pain with my hands shielding my face as I felt heavy boots against my chest and stomach, each kick harder and more brutal than the last.

"You fucked her, didn't you?" he shouted.

I couldn't talk; all I could do was groan in agony.

"You scumbag! I know you fucked her!"

I heard the bedroom door open and Stephanie approach. I saw only her feet. She tried pushing the man away while pleading with him to stop.

The last thought that registered in my mind, right before I lost consciousness, is that she called him Max and that she said it in a tender, almost loving way.

25

AS A CHILD I suffered multiple concussions.

When I was five, my father built me and my brother a bunk bed out of recycled timber. It was an ugly, rickety thing that creaked and wobbled. I was excited. I insisted on having the top bunk. There was only one problem: I'm not a peaceful sleeper. I tend to toss and turn, and since my father neglected to install a safety rail, at some point in the night the inevitable occurred: I rolled off the edge, hitting the floor with an almighty thump.

I recall screaming in agony and confusion just before I blacked out. Two weeks later and still no rail, it occurred again: another concussion.

Concussions don't get easier with age. They still hurt like hell, still leave you with a splitting headache. The only difference is that, as an adult, you worry more. You worry that maybe the damage is permanent; that your brain will never be the same again; that you'll be stupider, slower, more forgetful.

Luckily these fears weren't warranted in my case. My assailant, out of cowardice rather than compassion, didn't administer enough blows to cause any serious damage. The moment it occurred to him that he'd rendered me unconscious, he got scared and fled, speeding off into the night with engine roaring and headlights beaming.

I wasn't out for long, only a minute or two. When I awoke, the first thing I saw was Stephanie leaning over me with a concerned look on her face. She helped me up off the floor and lay me on the couch on my back, placing a pillow behind my head.

She found an icepack in the freezer and wrapped it in a towel and handed it to me. I applied it gently to my now swollen nose. It had stopped bleeding and the blood on my face and t-shirt was already starting to dry. Stephanie cleaned up the worst of the blood, dabbing at it with a wet cloth.

She suggested calling an ambulance, picking up her phone in preparation to do so. I insisted that an ambulance was unnecessary, so she escorted me to her car and drove me straight to the emergency department of the Deloraine Hospital.

At the hospital I was given immediate attention. Doctors and nurses scanned my brain, did x-rays. They found no evidence of bleeding or swelling in the skull. The only thing broken was my nose, which they splinted and bandaged. To be on the safe side, they kept me in the hospital for two days, monitoring me every few hours.

The first day at the hospital, Stephanie hovered near my bedside wearing a perpetually guilty expression. She kept asking me if I was okay, and was there anything she could get me? Water? Food? I'd get angry, tell her to leave, so she'd walk out the door, looking hurt. Thirty minutes later she'd return, exhibiting the same guilty expression and asking the same annoying questions.

On the morning of the second day, I snapped. I said I didn't need her help and that she ought to get home to her daughter. I wasn't being petulant but practical. I didn't see any point in her remaining by my bedside. Besides, I knew it was only guilt that was keeping her around; and her guilt, frankly, sickened me.

This time Stephanie lost her patience with me, raising her voice in frustration. "I'm just trying to help, okay? I've already said I'm sorry. Do you want me to say it again?"

"I don't need another apology," I replied. "Or an explanation. The facts of what happened are clear: you were upset because you were on the outs with your lover, and instead of dealing with it like an adult, you decided to drag me into your drama, using me as a rebound so that you wouldn't have to feel so alone."

She shrugged. "I admit it was stupid of me to get involved with the guy. His name's Max. We dated for a few months. He got kind of weird, a bit obsessive. He kept blowing up my phone, sometimes leaving forty, fifty messages a day, so I dumped him and blocked his number. I had no idea he was stalking me."

"You blocked his number, did you? Yet he called you while we were at the shack. How?"

"He called from a private number. I didn't know it was him when I took the call."

"Why did you even talk to him? Why not simply hang up?"

"He struggles with depression. He told me he was feeling suicidal. I couldn't ignore him, Chuck. Imagine if he had killed himself? I couldn't live with that. Could you?"

"It's obvious you still have feelings for the guy. What really pisses me off, though, is the fact that you told him where we were staying. Why?"

"I didn't. He found out through a mutual friend. And by the way, I don't have feelings for him any longer. Unless you count sympathy."

"I find that hard to believe."

"Look, I broke up with him months ago, long before you and I met. Has it been difficult emotionally? Sure. But I've been trying to put that chapter of my life behind me, and it's not as though I don't like your company. I thought you and I could at least have some fun together."

"I think you used me, Stephanie. I think you're still in love with Max. How do I know you didn't manufacture this whole crazy drama as a way to get Max's attention and make him jealous?"

She shook her head and laughed. "I know you're a writer, Chuck, but that's a bit paranoid and overly-imaginative even for you."

"Your boyfriend—sorry, ex-boyfriend, or so you claim—could've killed me, Stephanie."

She leaned forward, tried to reach for my hand. I pushed it away.

"Max was a bomb waiting to go off. He'll probably serve time in prison for what he did to you. Honestly I think it's the best thing for him. It'll force him to take responsibility for once and get his life in order."

"Fuck that guy. And fuck you for fucking him. I honestly hope he kills himself: one less philistine on the planet."

"Fine," said Stephanie, her face red with anger. "If that's how it's going to be, then fuck you too, Chuck."

On her way towards the door, she paused, tossing my car keys on the foot of the bed. "It's parked opposite the library."

And with that she was gone.

———

That afternoon, a police woman in her forties with short, sandy-coloured hair and a perpetually quizzical expression arrived to take a statement. I told her what I remembered of the incident and she told me what I already knew from my conversations with Stephanie: that my assailant had been charged with assault and was currently awaiting trial. She mentioned that during the trail I'd be required to attend court to give evidence against him.

She stood tall and erect, not once smiling. I had hoped that under her professional, steel-like exterior there might be some sensitivity in the woman, some slight trace of maternal warmth. Deep down I wanted her to comfort me, to tell me I'd been wronged and that everything would be okay. But she didn't. She came. She left. And that was it.

Once discharged from the hospital, I figured I'd stay in Deloraine for a few more days. I needed some time to rest to allow my injuries to heal. I still had a bandage over my nose and my left eye was black and bruised. My stomach was also bruised and sore. Mentally I wasn't in the best shape either. The world for me had become an ugly place and I wasn't yet prepared to face it.

I checked myself into the *Mountain View Inn*. It was cheap, only $87 a night, and instead of eating out I bought groceries from the nearby supermarket that required little to no cooking: instant noodles, fruit, cheese, salami, muesli bars. I was tempted to buy alcohol but didn't.

For the entire first day I didn't leave my bed. I spent my time sleeping, watching *YouTube* videos on my phone and reading the last few chapters of *Ask the Dust*. On the second day, I took long walks in the park and reflected on my life. I found myself thinking about Rinpoche and the years I'd spent living at the Buddhist retreat centre. In the process, some long-forgotten memories re-emerged.

26

IRONICALLY, MY MOTHER WAS attached to the notion that I become a Buddhist—ironically because, in Buddhist philosophy, it's recognised that attachment is the cause of all suffering.

Convinced I'd benefit from talking to Rinpoche, she arranged for me to have a personal meeting with the great man. At the time, I was still on the path to becoming a yogi, but so far my dick hadn't grown much bigger and I was beginning to lose hope that the daily cold showers and meditation sessions were having any noticeable impact on my chi.

Many sought Rinpoche's advice in relation to not only spiritual matters, but life in general. There was nothing he didn't know, no question he couldn't answer. He was an unending fount of wisdom. A single interaction or conversation with the man could change one's life forever and for the better. Or so his students believed.

Questions put to Rinpoche included: What breed of dog should I buy? What should I pursue as a career? What kind of person should I choose as a partner? and What's the best way to fix my lower-back pain?

Prior to my meeting with Rinpoche, I developed an explosive case of diarrhoea, visiting the toilet three times within the space of half-an-hour. The final visit was a close call: I nearly shat my pants.

When, finally, I entered his office, it was with a racing heart, sweaty palms and an ass sore from too much wiping. I felt anxious, impure, exposed, unworthy. Rinpoche enjoyed the company of pretty teenage girls, openly flirting with them, but I wasn't that.

His office was a small, windowless, square-shaped room illuminated by a single table lamp. The furnishings consisted of two armchairs, a rug and a coffee table. Attached to the ceiling was an antique metal fan that squeaked and rattled with each rotation.

Rinpoche sat waiting as I entered, looking calm and poised. He wore a purple satin shirt and black corduroy trousers, and for a moment I thought he looked almost pretty, like some effeminate prince from Tibet.

"Shall I close the door?" I asked.

He nodded as though the answer were obvious.

For several seconds I battled with the door; the wood was warped from the moisture and the heat and the bottom of it dragged along the ground.

The moment I sat down, a blowfly detached itself from the ceiling and began to buzz around chaotically. We watched it circle the room twice before landing on the tip of the fan.

"Hot day, isn't it?" I said, not sure how else to get the conversation started.

"It's the middle of summer," he replied. "What do you expect?"

I nodded. "Do you think we'll have bushfires this summer? Last year we did."

He looked at me as if I were dense, then shrugged. "A lot of things happened last year."

"True," I mumbled.

So far the meeting was going terribly. Here I was seated in the presence of a living Buddha and he'd already concluded that I was an idiot and not worth talking to. In truth, I didn't want to be here. I wanted to be alone in my room, curled up in my bed with a good book. I resented my mother for insisting I go through with this charade.

"So what's it like being a Rinpoche? Busy?"

He nodded, not making eye contact.

That the man didn't like me was evident. I was beneath him, not deserving of his time and attention. The rest of the meeting we spent in silence. When it was over, he calmly rose from his chair and opened the door to let me out.

————

When my mother asked me how the meeting went, I told her the truth: that it wasn't so much a meeting as a period of shared silence.

I detected on her face a hint of disappointment. "Rinpoche isn't like other spiritual teachers. He's part of the crazy wisdom tradition. He was silent because he was trying to teach you something."

"Teach me what? That I talk too much? I'm already pretty quiet as it is."

"No. He was teaching you about emptiness. You should be grateful."

After that I kept my distance from Rinpoche, or, more accurately, we kept our distance from each other. If I happened to run into him on the grounds of the retreat centre, I'd nod, mumble hello, and continue walking. I remained undecided as to whether or not he was truly a Buddha. Eventually I came to conclude that it didn't really matter. For, after all, I wasn't a Buddhist myself and had no intention of becoming one.

Fuck Buddhism, I decided.

27

TO AMUSE MYSELF, I continued to explore the Buddhist centre's many nooks and crannies. One time, quite by accident, I found a hidden room behind the women's shower block.

The shower block and the room in question was separated by a sturdy brick wall. The very top row of bricks had holes for ventilation. These holes were large enough and positioned at just the right height to allow a person situated on the other side of the wall to peer directly into the showers.

For a horny teenage boy, it was the ultimate find. To be able to look upon all that naked flesh—while remaining completely hidden—was a voyeur's dream come true, like something out of the movie *Porky's*.

I recall the day I first explored the room. It was accessible via a yellow door tucked away beneath the exterior kitchen stairs. Used for storage, it was packed with building materials: timber offcuts, old windows, fragments of drywall. Though technically part of the crawl space, there was sufficient height between the dusty ground below and the wooden floor above to enable one to walk around without having to stoop.

I was a genius for finding this place, I thought. Here I'd be able to view tits and ass to my heart's content and none would be the wiser. And yet there remained one catch: someone else was using this place for their own enjoyment. I wasn't the first.

I paused when I spotted it. Sat inverted against the wall was a maroon milk crate. I went over and stood on it. From this height, I was afforded a perfect view into the women's showers. The voyeur who frequented this place was well-prepared; he even had his own stool.

Looking around, I noticed something else. Directly above me, cut into the floor, was a square trapdoor, just wide enough for a slender person to crawl through. Mounted on hinges, it was currently shut and securely latched.

I was immediately hit with two realisations: first, whoever accessed this area did so not from outside but from the room above; and second, the room above was Rinpoche's private residence.

Was he the voyeur in question? The evidence at hand suggested as much. Like me he was below average in height, hence the milk crate. To say nothing of the highly suspicious position of the trapdoor.

The voyeur I never identified. The risk of being caught prevented me from ever revisiting the room. It's not that I wasn't a pervert and potential peeping tom; it's that I lacked the balls required to follow through with my plan.

One night I had a dream in which I found myself back in the secret room, lured there by lustful thoughts and the possibility of catching a glimpse of women showering. I discovered, however, that I wasn't alone. Someone had beaten me to it. A man.

He stood on the milk crate dressed in striped pyjamas, a wide grin on his deranged face. His pants and underwear sat bunched at his ankles, and in one hand he held his exposed cock, the thing wrinkled, flaccid and deformed. From his other hand swung an electric lantern, casting about the room a constantly shifting, eerie blue light.

I sensed he'd been expecting me. "Get your cock out," he demanded. "Let's wank. Let's wank together. The girls will be here soon."

The man was Rinpoche.

28

THE LAST TIME I saw Rinpoche I was twenty-eight years old and his body was on fire.

It was my mother who told me of his passing. Her call came one afternoon as I was wheeling the garbage bins down the driveway to be emptied the following day, a poetically fitting time to be informed of someone's death.

She didn't cry during the conversation, although the emotion in her voice was easy to detect, and that's saying a lot; rarely does my mother feel sad about anything.

Rinpoche's death, though untimely, came not as a surprise. For much of his life he'd suffered from poor health, and during the six months prior to his passing many had noticed a deterioration in his physical and mental well-being. He'd become a recluse, rarely leaving his house. His duties as a guru he'd all but renounced.

According to my mother, he'd suffered a heart attack at home in the early hours of the morning. An ambulance had been called but it arrived too late, and he'd died while lying helpless on the tiled kitchen floor, between the sink and the pantry, accompanied by his wife and one of the monks.

I attended his funeral out of a sense of obligation towards my mother, but mostly out of morbid curiosity and the chance to witness with my own eyes a cremation in the traditional, Tibetan Buddhist style.

His body—which was first wrapped in cloth— was burned inside a pyramidal structure called a stupa, using wood as the fuel. The front opening of the stupa was too narrow to permit a clear view of Rinpoche's burning corpse. This was as it should be; the guts can spill out when a body burns and it's not a pretty sight.

The smell, though it didn't overly bother me, wasn't pleasant: a bit like barbeque but with slightly rancid meat. The smoke, which was thick and black, got into my eyes and up my nose; and it disturbed me to know that I was breathing in particles of human corpse.

As part of the proceedings, prayers were chanted and pujas performed. The monks looked serious, austere. A no-nonsense bunch. Women sobbed quietly.

Almost half the local Tibetan community showed up. I noticed they looked very different to the Chinese, their skin a brownish-red. Some of the women wore traditional garb and they emanated a kind of wistful beauty. The men, on the other hand, were an intimidating bunch— macho, fierce, barrel-chested, capable of wrestling yacks with their bare hands. One of them glowered at me.

As a non-believer and known critic of the Buddhist community, I was wise to keep my distance from the crowd. I walked up the hill, found a patch of shade near a shed. Seated here in solitude with my back against the corrugated tin wall, I was overcome by the urge to say a prayer for the deceased:

"Sorry you died, Rinpoche. I didn't like you very much, but I didn't think you were a bad person either. These people think you're coming back, that you're going to be reincarnated, but I know that's just fantasy. You were just a man. You were born, you lived, you died. You had friends, family, hopes, dreams, desires. Your existence was finite as it is for every one of us. So long, brother."

29

—·—

IT WAS MY MENTAL rather than physical wellbeing that had suffered the greatest injury as a consequence of the assault. I was angry at my assailant, angry at Stephanie. I felt betrayed, lonely, unloved, a victim of a cruel and heartless world.

Late at night, unable to sleep, I indulged in dark fantasies in which I exacted revenge on Stephanie and her former lover. These thoughts became progressively violent and remained my only source of pleasure.

While having breakfast one morning in my motel room, my ex-wife called. She asked why I hadn't arrived as usual to pick up my son. Knowing it would bring her satisfaction—and inspire much gossip—to learn of my romantic misadventure, I lied and said I'd been injured by a falling branch from a gumtree. A ridiculous claim, though she seemed to believe it.

"You never did have much luck, did you, Chuck?" she said, her tone mocking.

"What's that supposed to mean?" I asked.

"Never mind. It's just a joke."

Outside it was sunny and the birds were busy. Through the glass I watched a scarlet robin land on the window sill. It cocked its head, looked at me. In seconds it was gone in a flutter of tiny wings.

"Could you at least pretend to have some sympathy? I have a broken nose for Christ's sake. It's not as though you had much compassion when we were married."

"How could I? You complained all the time. There was always something wrong with you. It was exhausting."

My porridge had grown cold and I'd lost my appetite. I pushed the bowl out of the way.

"That's how you feel about love, is it? Hard work?"

"I loved you once. I was a different person then. People change. Sorry."

I said nothing.

"Your problem, Chuck, is that you're stubborn. You want the world to be a certain way. But the world's not what you think it is. It's something else."

My throat felt clogged with emotion; I forced myself to speak. "It's something else alright. The world's a great big pile of shit."

"The world's the world. Deal with it."

There was a pause; then I said, "You're moving to Queensland, aren't you, taking our son with you?"

"How did you know?"

"I found the real estate agent's card."

"Oh. I was going to tell you."

"Why leave? Why take our son away?"

"It's best for me and it's best for our son. There are more opportunities in Queensland, that's all."

"You're good at taking care of number one. I'll give you that. I can think of several words for what you are: selfish, opportunistic, cold-hearted."

"Ha! As if I care what you think of me. The house is already on the market, by the way. The agent's expecting to receive an offer within the week."

"So that's it, then? I don't get to see my son?"

"If you give a shit about our son, move! For once in your life, fight for something."

The phone went silent; she'd hung up on me.

I stood up, and, holding the bowl of porridge in both hands as if it were a cream pie, I launched the fucking thing across the room. It hit the wall with a smash, a messy explosion of milky porridge and broken China.

30

AFTER FOUR DAYS OF hotel living, I decided it was time to hit the road and head home. The pain of my injuries was minimal at this point, not serious enough to prevent me from driving. I still looked ridiculous on account of the bandage over my nose, but, in all honestly, I was beyond caring.

Life, I'd concluded, was meaningless, a joke. Why should I give a damn about something as trivial as my appearance? Why should I give a damn about anything? The pessimists were right: the world is truly a bad place. The nihilists were right too: it's both bad and meaningless.

It was a sunny, cloudless morning as I set off. Everything seemed to be alive with beauty and heavy with the promise of spring. I passed cows grazing in paddocks of rich green grass, hedges, poplar trees, gumtrees, willows. It had long struck me as deeply paradoxical that the natural world, which God supposedly made and afterwards considered "good," ought to be so beautiful yet so filled with suffering.

What kind of God would create a sublime world, populate it with animals and humans, yet design the conditions of existence in such a way as to maximise the pain and suffering of the latter? The answer was obvious: only a sadist, only a torturer.

Animals, of course, were too dumb to suffer in an any meaningful way. Existential pain was beyond their capacity. Humans, on the other hand, were superbly designed to suffer. Create an entity with an ego, a sense of self, equip that entity with the ability to reflect on its own existence, including awareness of its unavoidable death, and you have a being capable of torturing itself with its own thoughts.

Nice one, Yahweh. Well done.

I was reminded of a quote by the philosopher Schopenhauer that, as a teenager, I'd committed to memory in order to sound smart when debating Christians: "If God made the world, I would not be that god, for the misery of the world would break my heart."

———

I was about half-way between Deloraine and Devonport, cruising at high speed along the highway, when I heard the familiar "flapp-flapping" sound of loose rubber and detected the loss of traction typical of a punctured rear tyre.

I swore out loud, banged the steering wheel with a fist. I only just managed to restrain myself from screaming. This was the last thing I needed. I wondered if God, having heard my blasphemous thoughts, had decided to punish me.

I pulled over onto the shoulder of the road, switched off the engine. For a minute I sat there with my head in my hands, reluctant to face the situation.

Directly adjacent was a ramshackle farmhouse, its blinds drawn tight. I was partly blocking their driveway, not that this seemed to be a problem; I'd change the tyre and be gone within a matter of minutes.

Having gathered the jack and spare from the trunk, I quickly got to work. I jacked up the rear of the car, loosened and removed each lug nut with the wrench, then finally lifted off the punctured tyre.

I was about to mount the spare on the wheel studs when, in my clumsiness and haste, I slipped. One moment I was holding the spare; the next moment it was rolling away at tremendous speed, straight down the farmhouse's steep dirt driveway.

It was in the grip of gravity now, out of control and unstoppable. In its path was a thick patch of blackberry vines. I watched the spare plough straight through the tangle of thorny canes and leaves, before being lost to view.

Fucking great. Now I'd have to go in there and retrieve it while trying my best not to get cut and scratched; and since this was private land, I'd first need to obtain permission from whoever lived here.

As I knocked on the door of the farmhouse it was with the expectation that I'd soon be looking into the vacant eyes of some inbred yokel. In my mind I heard the strumming of banjos and hoped that my regular sessions at the gym had improved my running speed and endurance.

I heard footfalls; then the door creaked open; then I saw a face. She must've been about sixty, although she looked for her age extremely healthy and dare I say, quite pretty. She had curly, dark hair, hazel eyes and olive skin.

She seemed unphased by my appearance, paying little attention to my bandaged nose.

"Sorry to bother you," I said, "but I lost my spare tyre in the tangle of blackberry vines on your property."

"Let me get my husband," she said, in an accent I couldn't quite place

A moment later her husband emerged. A short, balding man with a round face, he reminded me of the actor Danny DeVito. He stood there in silence with an expression of wry amusement as he listened to my account of the lost spare tyre.

"Let's go get your wheel," he said.

I followed him down a garden path to a small tin shed. He rummaged around in the dim interior among greasy tools, dusty fuel drums, and plastic storage boxes, finally locating two pairs of gardening gloves. He donned one pair and threw the other in my direction. They flopped at my feet. I put them on.

Into a wheelbarrow he loaded rakes, mattocks, hedge shears and secateurs, and we pushed it down the hill to the blackberry pile. The spare tyre I couldn't see, although I knew it was buried somewhere in that mountain of tangled vines.

Gesturing to the vines, the old man said, "First you help me clear them. Then we find your wheel."

I felt like slapping him in the face. It would take an hour to clear the vines, maybe longer. All of this work just to get my spare back? Hardly a fair exchange.

"I'm on a tight schedule," I lied. "I've got to be at a friend's wedding this afternoon. Can't I just go in there and get it?"

"Easy job," he laughed. "Won't take long."

I sighed and got to work. For well over an hour we clipped, hacked, and dug at the blackberry vines, loading the trimmings into the wheelbarrow and dumping them in a nearby pile. It was a back-breaking task. Sweat poured from my body, dampening the armpits and front of my shirt. My muscles ached and scratches from thorns covered my arms.

As we were taking a short break, the old woman emerged from the house with a tray bearing a stack of tuna and mayonnaise sandwiches, along with tall glasses of lemonade with ice. We ate and drank without speaking, then immediately returned to the task at hand.

Once we were done, where the blackberry vines had flourished was now flat soil with a few clumps of roots poking through the surface. Luckily, the spare was easy to locate and had survived its journey down the hill unscathed. The old man insisted on helping me attach it, so together we rolled it to the car.

As we were crouched beside each other tightening the nuts on the wheel studs, he turned to me and asked, "Do you have a family?"

I shook my head. "No, but I have a son."

"Divorced?"

"Yes."

He nodded in understanding. "And what do you do with yourself?"

"I'm a writer."

"Ah, this explains why the wheel got away from you."

I laughed. "I'm no mechanic, that's for sure."

"Can you cook?"

"No. My cooking's terrible."

"Maybe you need help. Maybe you need to find a new wife."

"I can't see that happening anytime soon."

"Why not?"

I told him what I'd been through with Stephanie. By the time I was finished, I was feeling sorry for myself and on the verge of crying.

"And you regard this as a bad thing?" asked the old man. "An unlucky thing?"

"Of course. How was it anything different?"

"I see it as a foolish thing. Some women... not so good. If you chase that kind of woman, always a price. Everything has a price. Things balance out."

"Not in my case. I ended up with a broken nose. I ended up with nothing."

"Yet you slept with her. Used her body. Pleasure in exchange for pain." He pointed to my bandaged nose.

"Sure." The old man had a point and this I was compelled to acknowledge.

"My wife, she no longer sleeps with me. We don't talk much either. But we keep each other company."

The wheel was now attached. We both stood up, leaning against the side of the car.

"How long have you been married?"

"Forty years."

"That's quite an achievement. Well done."

He laughed. "Don't congratulate me. It's been hard work. That wife of mine, she isn't easy to live with."

"You strike me as someone who's had a good life. Tell me: what's the secret to finding happiness?"

He pondered the question for a long time; then he said, "Happiness can't be found, that's the secret. If you're lucky, patient, it will find you. But it won't be happiness the way most people think of happiness."

"I think happiness is a myth. We're born, we suffer, we die, and that's it."

He shrugged as though in defeat. "I know nothing. I'm just a simple farmer. Thirty years ago I move to Australia. I work hard, buy land, raise children."

"Your point being?"

"My point is that I think you expect too much. Young people especially, they want everything. They're selfish. They ignore responsibility, sacrifice. They ignore their debt to God."

"So you're a Christian then? You know, when you Christians start preaching about our debt to God, that's when I tend to tune out."

"Forget the word 'God.' I'm talking about faith."

"So you're saying I'm supposed to believe in God without any proof of his existence?"

"No. You can have faith without belief."

"How? That makes no sense."

"Faith comes down to trust." He gave the spare tyre a kick with his boot. "Did you have faith you'd get your wheel back after helping me clear the blackberry vines? Did you trust me?"

I shrugged. "Sure. In all honesty, though, I didn't want to help you."

"Why did you then?"

"Because I thought it was the right thing to do."

"That's faith. Today you had faith. Did your faith serve you?"

"I suppose."

Looking into my eyes, he extended his hand. I extended mine and we shook.

"I believe you can have a good life, Chuck. But it's going to require faith. Start by having faith in yourself. Now I should let you go. You have a wedding to attend, yes?"

I nodded, turned, and was about to open the door of the car when my conscience made me pause. I looked back at the old man. "I lied about the wedding. I'm sorry. There is no wedding."

The old man smiled, then broke out laughing. It poured out of him, arising from a place deep in his chest.

I said goodbye, climbed into my car, and seconds later I was back on the highway heading home.

About the Author

Louis Proud is an Australian author of both fiction and non-fiction whose work explores such diverse themes as existentialism, masculinity, religion and the unexplained. He makes his home by the sea.